The Valentine's Date

By B. N. Hale

27 Dates: The Series

Table of Contents

Volume 27: The Valentine's Date

Chapter 1

Reed Hanson leaned back in his chair and stared at the calendar on the wall of his office. Again. He'd left Boulder Colorado three weeks ago but it felt like a lifetime, and he now counted the hours until he could talk to Kate. For nearly a year the dating challenge had dominated his life, a persistent source of excitement as he and Kate had traded being in charge, each date surpassing expectations. But things had changed when he'd moved to New York City.

The internship that had taken him to New York was a golden opportunity that would propel him into any career, any doctoral program. Short of picking a fight with one of the doctors, he could all but guarantee a future counseling practice anywhere in the country. It was a dream job, but he hoped it didn't cost him his dream girl.

His office was larger than he'd expected and contained a wide oak desk with a comfortable office chair. The dark wood of the desk matched the built-in bookshelves in the corner and the intricate moulding along the walls. A large TV was hidden behind a section of paneling and was accessible with a remote, allowing him to display information from his computer. It was the nicest room he'd ever occupied but paled in comparison to the rest of the institute.

Large and containing a two-level lobby, the institute was home to seven psychologists and psychiatrists, doctors who served the needs of socialites, politicians, and celebrities. Reed had studied the files and been shocked by the clientele.

He sighed and leaned back in his chair. The institute was everything he'd dreamed of, yet each day he felt a measure of dread as he joined the three other interns for the short cab ride to the building. He knew it was because he missed Kate, and his gaze once again returned to the calendar, to the date one week away. February 14th. It had been one year since Kate's roommates had set them up on Valentine's Day. One year since the start of the dating challenge. To his surprise he'd fallen for Kate, and he'd fallen hard.

There was a knock at the door and Reed straightened. "Come in."

Hannah swung the door open while balancing a large package in her hands. With dark hair and golden brown eyes, Hannah was stunningly attractive. She had an athletic and graceful build, her clothing enhancing her curves. She was also one of the other three interns, and made little effort to hide her attraction for Reed.

Unfortunately, Dr. Dickson had asked them both to work on a major research project, an extension of Reed's thesis. Each day Reed and Hannah spent the morning exploring the city, planning dates for institute patients. Reed kept both an emotional and physical distance from Hannah, but the task was made difficult when their bedrooms were adjacent and part of his job was to take her on fake dates.

"What's that?" Reed asked, eyeing the package.

"Something you've been waiting on," she said. "It actually arrived a couple of days ago, but I wanted to add my touch."

Curious, he came around the desk to the table where she placed the box. Her smile was excited as he pulled the tape and opened cardboard. Peering inside, he realized it was some sort of frame, so he caught the edge and slid it free. Inside the expensive frame lay a single document, the formal script detailing his previous school and his name.

Seeing his master's diploma elicited a surge of pride. In a flood of memories he recalled all the classes and homework, the late night study sessions and the hundreds of essays. He smiled and ran his hand along the glass above his name, the frame having obviously been added by Hannah.

"You didn't have to do this," he said.

"Someone needed to," she said.

Framing his diploma represented a kind gesture, but from Hannah it made him a touch uncomfortable. She had a talent for inserting herself

8

into his life in ways that made it hard for him to refuse. Still, he couldn't be upset at such a gift.

"Thank you," Reed said, admiring the frame.

"Jackson forwarded it here and I saw it in the mail. I hope you don't mind."

"Not at all."

She flashed her dazzling smile. "Least I could do. Do you need help to hang it . . .?"

"I think I can manage," Reed said, and glanced to the wall behind his desk, where a pair of nails had been when Reed had arrived, presumably left by the former occupant. "I do know my way around a hammer."

She put her hand on his arm. "You should be proud of yourself."

He shifted his feet, subtly breaking the contact, and she withdrew. If she noticed his effort to retreat she gave no sign, and instead asked him about dinner. They were supposed to go out with the other interns but Reed abruptly decided against it.

"I actually need to take care of something," he said. "Maybe tomorrow?"

"I'll hold you to that," Hannah said with a smile, and then left.

When the door shut, Reed shook his head. Hannah was beautiful and there were many interests they shared. If he had never met Kate, he might have been attracted to Hannah, but not now. The problem was getting Hannah to recognize his heart already belonged to Kate.

There was a knock at the door and he swung it open. "Hannah, I don't . . ."

But it was Dr. Dickson standing in the opening. Tall and thin, he had dark hair that was going silver, giving him a distinguished air. He spoke in a melodic bass, his voice inviting trust with every syllable.

He offered a slight smile. "Mr. Thompson, were you expecting Ms. Davenport?"

"No, sorry," Reed said. "Please come in."

Even after three weeks he found it disconcerting to be treated as an equal. Reed had expected the internship to be a lot of grunt work, but the doctors treated the interns with respect, probably because most had been interns themselves at one point.

Dr. Dickson accepted a seat and motioned Reed to his. "Are you busy?"

"Did I forget a session with a client?" Reed asked.

"No," he said. "The Youngs canceled their session and I thought I'd take advantage of the moment to speak with you."

"About the research project?"

"That too."

Reed frowned, confused by Dr. Dickson's smile. "You have me intrigued," he said.

Dr. Dickson sidestepped the topic. "Your morning excursions have been very insightful, and your reports are quite detailed. What is your impression of the city?"

Reed settled back in his chair. "I think I could spend a decade planning dates for couples and still not discover everything the city has to offer."

"Do you have enough that I can write a date prescription?" Dr. Dickson's lips twitching with amusement.

Reed hesitated, mentally listing all the locations that he and Hannah had explored. They'd visited places to eat and searched for activities, many of which were not obvious. They'd spent hours discussing ideas on how to enhance the events in order to bring out the romance.

"I think we're read," he said.

"I'd like the Youngs to be the first test case," Dr. Dickson said. "They've both agreed to try a date so I want you to plan one. Use their file and work with Hannah. I'll need to confirm the final plan when you're finished."

"Of course," Reed said.

Dr. Dickson caught sight of the diploma on the table and motioned to it. "It won't be long before you have a doctorate to go beside that one. Have you given thought to which school you'd like to attend?"

"A little," Reed said. "But I've been more focused on getting a handle on things here."

"My niece wants to go to Harvard."

"Elaina?" Reed asked. "I met her at the benefit last week."

Dr. Dickson nodded his approval. "She's more interested in disorders than family counseling, but I can't fault her for that." He smiled. "I'm taking her to dinner today, actually to one of the places on your recommendation list."

"An uncle-niece date?" Reed asked, feigning dismay. "I didn't realize I needed to plan those."

"Perhaps," Dr. Dickson smiled. "You never know when you might need it. Her father passed away last year, so once a month I take Elaina out to continue his tradition."

"That's kind of you," Reed said.

As they talked, Reed wondered what Dr. Dickson's real purpose was. In three weeks he'd shown remarkable efficiency, managing the demands on his time so well that he rarely had to work late.

"How are things going with Ms. Davenport?" he finally asked.

"Very well," Reed said, choosing his words carefully. "We work well together."

Dr. Dickson was not fooled. "It's clear she has feelings for you."

"I suspect she does," he replied. "But I can assure you it will not affect our work."

Dr. Dickson chuckled to himself. "One of my favorite things about you is your candor, and you do not realize what a gift it is. I think I will return the favor. Lately I've seen couples part ways more often than they stay together. The reasons are varied and many, but they do have one thing in common. Distraction. Husband or wife it makes no difference, but if they are significantly distracted by outside influences, divorce becomes a real possibility. I had thought you and Hannah to be a perfect pairing to research how we can improve the lives of our clients, but I am concerned her attraction towards you could be problematic for our study."

Reed recognized the unspoken question. Dr. Dickson wanted to determine if their working together would adversely impact the study, as well as their work overall. It was an opening query to measure Reed's reaction to Hannah.

"We can remain professional," Reed said.

"Are you certain?"

Reed smiled and swept a hand to the files on his desk. "I am just as eager as you to see this research put into practice."

"Excellent." His eyes sparkled with sudden mischief as he rose to his feet. "I know the last few weeks have been difficult, so you can take the rest of the day to yourself."

Reed glanced to the burnished bronze clock on the wall. It was just after two, and getting off this early was unheard of. He frowned and returned his gaze to Dr. Dickson, who'd stepped to the door.

"Is this another test?" he asked.

"I think you would call this a game," he said, his smile turning mischievous. "But I cannot claim to be the creator." He reached into his suit coat and removed an envelope, which he placed on the table. "Enjoy the rest of your day." He smiled and patted it before slipping out the door.

Reed rose and approached the table. The envelope was regular business size and it had obviously been mailed. It was addressed to Dr. Dickson. Then Reed noticed the sender and his heart skipped against his ribs. Kate. It was already open, so he removed a single sheet of paper. On it was an address and a time for later that day, as well as a brief message.

Will you fly with me?

Kate

He smiled as he read the note, the weight of the past three weeks lifting like an anvil had been removed from his shoulders. Picking up his phone, he shut his laptop and walked into the lobby of the office. Hannah's office was across from his and she was stretching in her chair. She spotted Reed with his laptop bag on his shoulder and raised an eyebrow.

"Where are you off to?" she asked.

Reed's smile widened. "I have a date," he said, already putting his phone to his ear.

He should not have been pleased by the slight frown creasing her features, but he was. Then he slipped out the door and took the elevator down. As he stepped outside the ringing ended, and he heard Kate's voice.

Chapter 2

"Hello?"

Reed's smile seemed to fill his whole body. "Kate," he drawled. "Did you send my boss a letter?"

"Maybe," she replied, her tone mischievous.

He laughed as he turned up the street. "Why did you think he would let me go early?"

"The envelope contained a second letter," she said. "When I met him he did say he wanted *me* to win the dating challenge, so I wrote a letter asking him to join my side."

Reed shook his head, marveling at Kate's bold ingenuity. At the start of their dating challenge they'd enlisted each other's roommates, and then the pool of allies had quickly grown to include family members, friends, even professors. But Reed had never expected her to reach out and ask Dr. Dickson for help on a date—or for him to accept.

"In August you asked if I'd fall for you," he said, looking for a cab, but none were visible. "Are you going to make me drop a hundred feet again?"

"As I recall, I let you take the blindfold off," she said.

He checked his phone and realized he had time to walk home. The last few weeks had been freezing but today was warmer, topping fifty degrees for the first time. Sunlight filtered through the trees growing along the sidewalk, brightening the street and reflecting off the cars.

The upscale neighborhood was home to many offices, its location just a block from the brownstone neighborhoods. Rather than take a taxi, Reed turned up the street, intent on walking the eight blocks to the brownstone he and the other interns shared.

Kate proved cagey about the date, but just the prospect of an afternoon talking to her lifted his spirits. He reached his house and hurried up the stairs to his room, replacing his suit with more comfortable clothes. Then he took a taxi north.

"849 Ridge Hill Boulevard, Yonkers," Reed said, giving the address she'd provided in the letter.

The cabbie nodded and pulled into traffic. The traffic was lighter than normal, probably due to the hour, and it was also the first time he was going north. As they passed a tour bus, Reed resisted the urge to Google the address.

"Don't look up the address," Kate said.

Reed burst into a laugh. "I was just thinking that."

"You've never ruined the surprise before," she said. "Don't start now."

"I promise," he said, and then spotted an ad for flowers and chocolates. "Hey, did you see that next week is Valentine's Day?"

"That's not the sort of thing a girl forgets."

He grunted in amusement. "True, but this has a little more significance for us. Does it count as our one year anniversary? Or do we count that from when we first kissed?"

"Two anniversaries," she said. "One from when we first met, and one from when we started dating for real."

"Done," he said. "Then what are we doing for Valentine's Day?"

"That's up to you," she replied. "Today is my date. Next week is yours."

A slow smile spread on his face. "Then I get to end the dating challenge."

"*I* was supposed to end it," she protested. "That's what today is for."

He shook his head and then realized she couldn't see the motion. "Nope," he replied. "Today is the challenge date from last week that I missed—"

"—because you were on a date with Hannah," she said.

He grinned and then shared what Dr. Dickson had said. Reed would have thought she'd be upset by the revelation, but instead she found it amusing as well, and both agreed that Dr. Dickson believed they could keep Hannah out of their relationship.

He heard a car door open and shut. "Where are you going?"

"Same place as you," she said. "Except mine is in Denver."

The idea of them both doing the same activity—at the same time yet thousands of miles apart—brought a smile to his lips. Kate didn't say it, but she'd spent countless hours doing her own research, planning a date they could do despite the distance.

The cab driver leaned out and shouted at someone who'd cut him off, but Reed didn't care about the delay. He had Kate on the phone and an afternoon with her. Nothing else mattered. Kate too, seemed unfettered, and he settled into his seat to enjoy the ride.

An hour after leaving Reed's apartment, the cab driver pulled into a parking lot. A glance at the fare revealed it would be the most expensive ride he'd had since arriving in New York, so he resolved to take the subway back. He paid and thanked the driver and then got out, lifting his gaze to the sign on the building.

IFly Indoor Skydiving

"Really?" he asked.

She giggled. "You said you'd never go skydiving. I figured this would be the closest you'd get."

16

"Sometimes I think I'm dating a super villain," he said.

"You and me both," she said. "But I'm still a few minutes away. Do you mind waiting until I get there?"

He took a seat on the steps outside and watched a group of young teens walk out the door. Exuberant and laughing, they talked about their flights. Reed noticed all of their hair was messed up, either from the wind or the helmets he couldn't be sure.

A large banner outside the building showed a circular chamber with a powerful fan in its base. The wind lifted a smiling girl into the air, her blue suit holding her aloft on the current of air as another suited girl floated next to her, rising to join her level.

"Am I going to like this?" he asked.

"It's better than actually skydiving," Kate said. "All the fun without the fear."

"Would your brothers agree with that?" Reed asked.

"No," she said. "But they aren't going with us. When you get used to this, we'll do it for real."

"I'm not going to jump out of a plane." Reed shuddered at the idea. He didn't mind heights, but being that high was a class all its own.

She grunted as if she'd just had an idea. "I'll just ask Bake to help. He'll get it done."

Reed knew exactly what she meant by "get it done." Kate's oldest brother was in the military—special forces. The first night Reed had met the giant, he'd kidnapped him and gotten him into a knife fight. If Kate asked, Bake would be only too happy to drug him, kidnap him, and wake him up as he exited the plane.

"You're being overly dramatic," she laughed when he shared the thought.

"I'm not," he said. "We both know it's true."

"Maybe I'll ask Tyler for help," she relented.

"He's still in the Air Force," Reed said. "On a separate, unrelated note, I'd like to point out that I really like your brothers and respect them a great deal."

"Why would you say that?" she asked, and he heard her turn off her car.

"In case they're listening to this call."

She laughed. "I'm here. You ready to fly?"

"If I say no, would I still have to do it?"

"Yes."

"Then let's go!"

She laughed again and they both entered their respective buildings. His arrival was expected, his package of two flights already paid for. As they suited up, Reed transferred the call to his rarely used Bluetooth and then donned the helmet.

"Can you hear me?" he asked.

"Right here," she said, her voice sounding like she was right next to him.

He listened to the safety briefing, both in his room and through the Bluetooth. Dressed in the special flight suit and having signed the waver saying he wouldn't sue them if he died, he walked into the flight chamber.

"*Wow*," he breathed.

A woman was floating in the chamber, spinning effortlessly. The machine emitted a dull roar that was muted somewhat by the helmet, but his attention was on the flying woman.

Her suit looked custom, her helmet personalized with a falcon logo. She flipped upside down and then soared upward, her head pointed straight down as she glided around the walls. Then she flipped into the splits and spun on a central axis. She moved with such grace that she could have been flying of her own willpower.

"Don't think you're going to be doing that," the instructor at his side said. "She's the best of the instructors."

"I'm just hoping to keep my bones intact," Reed said.

He smirked. "Good goal, and as long as you listen to her, you'll be fine."

As he walked away Reed lowered his voice and spoke to Kate. "Did you hear that? Breaking my neck is a real possibility."

"Are you nervous?" she asked, and he could hear the smile in her voice.

"More excited than nervous," he said. "But this doesn't mean I'm jumping out of an airplane."

She laughed and then the instructor beckoned him forward. He climbed the steps to the door and the woman inside floated to the edge of the chamber, her feet dropping to the floor. The enormous fan slowed and they opened the door, allowing him inside.

"Don't worry," the woman said. "Hold my hands at first and keep your body flat."

"Are you holding another girl's hand?" Kate asked.

"If I have to," Reed said, responding to both of them.

He stepped out onto the grate above the fan, a thrill of excitement climbing up his chest. The air churned and flowed about him, ready to blast him off the grate and lift him into the air. The woman, whose tag he now read as Brooke, caught his hands and nodded to the instructor outside the cage.

"Take it slow," she called as the fan accelerated.

A nervous grin spread on Reed's face as the air powered up, gradually mounting until it felt like he was going to rocket up the chamber. Brooke leaned forward and hopped, flattening her body and rising off the floor. Straightening, she returned to the standing position before motioning to him.

Gripping her hand, he leaned forward and attempted the same motion. The air slammed into his chest, lifting him off the ground and sending him sideways. She expertly pushed his hands and stepped to his side, redirecting his motion so he stayed relatively horizontal.

The fan picked up speed and he rose into the air. He instinctively brought his hands inward. Doing so caused him to drop and Brooke pulled his arm out. For several tense seconds he struggled to keep his body stationary on a bubble of screaming air, until for one glorious moment, he succeeded.

Kate's cry of exultation sounded in his ear and he grinned. He imagined her in the same position, floating on air as another instructor held her, gently directing her to stay horizontal while wind battered her frame.

He began to laugh, the sheer excitement of flying mingling with the image of Kate doing the same. They may have been worlds apart, but he could hear her breathing, harsh and quick in his ear, and her instructor shouting a word of encouragement that matched Brooke's tone. They may have been apart, but it seemed she flew at his side.

"This is incredible!" he shouted.

Kate's response matched his own, and for a single instant, there was no distance. Time and space could not keep them apart, and even gravity lost its might to a stronger power, to what linked Reed to Kate. For the first time in three weeks, he felt whole.

Chapter 3

Kate listened to Reed through her earpiece. His laugh lifted her soul just as the blast of wind lifted her body. She'd gone skydiving with her brothers before and knew how to position her body, but it was different here. Still, she managed not to launch herself into the wall.

Outside the barrier, Ember and Marta, two of her roommates, waited for their turn. Kate had wanted to drive herself down to Denver, but as soon as her roommates had heard what she was doing, they'd insisted on accompanying her, ostensibly so she would not need to drive alone. It didn't matter, she was here with Reed.

It felt odd to feel so close to someone on the other side of the country, but it was an emotion she yearned for. She'd done her best to keep Reed from knowing the depths of her doubts regarding Hannah. The girl was a shark.

Kate's distraction cost her and the wind pushed her towards the wall. Her instructor managed to catch her and swing her back to the center, smiling as he kept her in form. He gave an approving nod when she righted herself and she resolved to not think about Hannah right now, not on a date with Reed.

She spun and twisted, the instructor retreating when she proved she could keep herself in control. Reed gave a very childlike shout of exuberance, the sound reminding her of the first time she went parachuting with her brothers. She wished Reed was in the room with her, but for now, it was enough that they were together.

"Do you have any idea how much I miss you?" Kate asked.

He laughed. "We're three weeks into our year apart. I miss you like crazy, but the time is flying."

Not on my end.

She didn't say it. Unwilling to puncture his happiness, she merely responded in kind, and the usually very perceptive Reed didn't notice the hesitation in her voice. She couldn't blame him. She had planned this date to be fun.

They finished their flights at almost the same moment, both exited for a break. She righted herself and the instructor guided her to the opening. Then he motioned to Ember, who approached the opening with her usual fearlessness.

"That was epic," Reed breathed.

Reed was not prone to outbursts of emotion so to hear such elation brought a smile to Kate's lips. Her previous doubt subsided and she was swept up in the moment of excitement, both reliving what they'd done.

"I wish I could watch you," Kate said.

"I think I can manage that," Reed said. "We can video call and I'll have someone hold it for me.

"I wouldn't be able to talk to you," she said.

"True," he replied. "But we did one with us talking, let's try one where we can see each other."

Kate hesitated, unwilling to reveal the fact that she'd brought two of her roommates on a date with Reed. Still, the temptation to watch him in the air machine was too much to resist, so she agreed and muted the phone to warn Marta.

"Don't let him know you're holding the phone," she said.

"I'm here with Ember," Marta said with a sniff. "I don't even know you."

Kate grinned and unmuted the phone before accepting the video call. Careful to keep the screen pointed away from Marta and the chamber, where Ember was flailing, she smiled when Reed's face resolved into view.

"That helmet is very fetching," Reed said, his voice barely audible over the droning machine.

Kate shook her head. "It looks better on you."

Reed looked away and then nodded. "Looks like it's my turn again. Want to watch me first?"

The screen slanted as he handed the screen to the guy on the bench, who Reed called Jason. The teenager was young, just out of his teens, and sported glasses and a hint of a mustache. Reed had apparently already asked him because he dutifully turned the screen to face the chamber as Reed got in.

Reed was athletic and flexible, but indoor skydiving required practice. Still, he managed to float of the ground well enough that the instructor let go. He rotated a little and gave a thumb's up to Kate, the action sending him sideways.

"He's doing good," Marta murmured.

"Maybe someday we can do it together," she said.

Marta snorted and Kate realized the second meaning of the statement. She flushed. "I didn't mean it that way."

"That's the way I took it," the teenager said, briefly turning the phone to him.

"Thanks Jason," Marta said sarcastically.

The kid grinned and turned the phone camera back toward the chamber, and Kate muted her phone so Jason wouldn't be able to hear any more. She gave a sour laugh and leaned back on the bench, wondering if they were right.

"You really think that's what it is?"

"Isn't it obvious?" Marta asked. "You haven't slept with him, so you wonder if your relationship is really as strong as you think. Don't worry. It is."

"You're not concerned about Hannah?"

Marta shook her head. "She's a predator, but Reed's not exactly easy prey. Before he met you, how many girls did he turn down?"

"Lots," Ember said, exiting the chamber. She removed her helmet and shook her bright red hair loose. "But Kate has unlocked his heart, and now that it's open . . ."

Marta jerked her head in disagreement. "There's no way Reed would cheat on Kate."

"It's not cheating if they are already broken up."

Kate listened to her friends argue, torn between both perspectives. Both were in agreement that Reed would not cheat, but that was where their opinions diverged, with Ember thinking Reed would drift away, break up, and then start dating Hannah. Marta and Brittney were both adamant that Reed would remain faithful, but Kate wasn't sure if that was because they really believed it, or *wanted* to believe.

"Reed's coming back," Kate said, gesturing to the phone.

The girls went silent and Kate unmuted the phone. Mercifully, Jason did not speak to Reed as he accepted the phone. Then Reed removed his helmet, brushing his hand through his black hair. Heat sparked in Kate's stomach and she wondered if Marta was right.

"Now I get to watch you fly," Reed said with a grin.

Kate handed the phone to Marta and then strode to the door, arriving as another person exited. The instructor beckoned her inside and she carefully pushed herself onto the bubble of air. Highly conscious of the fact that Reed was watching, she kept her motions small and fluid, but after a moment she realized she was attempting to look sexy.

She swallowed and inwardly laughed before focusing on her hands and legs, careful to direct the motion around her, feel the air press her

24

one way, and then another. It was strangely exciting to feel Reed's eyes on her and it pushed her to new heights. She dared to twist and turn in ways she would not have risked before. When the instructor finally called her down she marveled that even a country away, Reed still elicited a sense of courage.

The instructor followed her out and removed his helmet, revealing thick brown hair and startling green eyes. The tag on his chest revealed his name to be Kyle. His smile was rakish and attractive, and he spoke with a British accent.

"You're a natural."

"Thanks," she said, and tried to step away. She glanced to the phone but noticed Marta had surreptitiously turned the camera away.

"Do you live here in Denver?" he asked, following her as Kate removed her helmet and shook her brown hair free.

"Boulder, actually," she said, annoyed that he was so attractive.

His eyes lit up. "I just transferred there from the campus here in Denver."

"We live close to the Target," Ember supplied helpfully, and Kate shot her an annoyed look.

"I'll be living on ninth," he said. "Looks like we'll be close."

"Maybe we'll see you around." Kate extricated herself and collected the phone from Marta. She walked down the stairs, retreating as her roommates continued to talk to the too-friendly Kyle.

"Your cameraman was terrible," Reed said when Kate turned the camera on her and unmuted it.

"Camera*woman*," Kate corrected. "But she got distracted by the instructor, who was annoyingly handsome."

"I noticed," Reed said. "And did I catch a British accent?"

"I didn't notice," Kate said with a light laugh. She wondered how much he'd heard before Marta had muted the phone.

Reed grunted in amusement. As she pushed her way into the changing room she glanced back and found Kyle's eyes on her, the contact sparking a note of guilt in her chest. She was worried about Hannah but here she was, checking out another guy.

"What's next on the agenda?" Reed asked, also stepping into the changing room.

"You'll find out after we're changed," Kate said, shoving Kyle from her thoughts. She noticed another girl getting dressed and frowned. "I'll call you after."

"Deal," Reed said, and nodded to someone out of view. "But don't take too long." He flashed the smile she'd grown to love and she melted a little. "I'm excited for the rest of our date."

Kate agreed and hung up, and then changed quickly. When she was dressed in her normal clothes she gathered her coat and exited the room to the foyer of the structure. A group of Denver students were all crowding into the room, the press of bodies obscuring her view until she reached the exit. She descended the steps and pulled out her phone, but slowed when she spotted Ember and Marta talking to Kyle.

Dressed in fashionable jeans, a grey, long sleeved shirt, and leather jacket, Kyle looked like he'd been plucked from a magazine. A pair of girls that walked by almost drooled. Confused why he was with them, Kate joined her roommates and nodded to Kyle.

"Your roommates say you're in the engineering program," Kyle said, turning to Kate.

"I am," she replied.

"I'm doing aviation," he said. "I'd like to be a pilot like my dad. He was in the military in England."

"Kate's brothers are in the military here," Ember supplied, and Kate glared at her behind Kyle's back.

Unperturbed, Ember smiled. "We should get together," Ember said. "Maybe tonight at our place?"

"Sounds great," Kyle said, shouldering his duffel bag.

As Ember blithely handed over their address and phone number, Kate tried to keep her irritation in check. Kyle departed with a smile and strode to his car, a sleek BMW. The moment he pulled away Kate rounded on her roommates.

"What do you think you're doing?"

"He's clearly into you," Ember said, folding her arms. "And he's *really* hot."

"So?" Kate asked. "I'm in love with Reed."

"Love is a battlefield," Ember reasoned. "And you need your own Hannah."

As Marta hid a smile, Kate scowled and tried to keep the surge of vindication from taking root. The prideful part wanted to shove Kyle in Reed's face so he'd know what it felt like, and she was grateful that voice was not strong enough to win.

"This isn't going to work," Kate said.

"We'll see," Ember said, walking around her jeep and climbing in.

Kate turned on Marta. "Why would you support this?"

"Because Ember is right," Marta said. "You need your own Hannah."

"I'm not quitting on Reed."

"I know," Marta said. "But Reed needs to see the *risk*."

Kate scowled and looked away. Taking her silence as agreement, Marta smirked and climbed into the car. Kate's phone, forgotten in her hand, began to buzz and she saw that it was Reed. She glanced to the empty spot where Kyle had been parked, and a slow smile spread on her face.

Chapter 4

Kate talked to Reed the entire drive back to Boulder, trying to ignore her roommates. The two spoke in whispers so as to avoid Reed catching on, but the talk grew increasingly racy the longer they drove. As they got off the exit in Boulder she had to silence her phone in order to silence them, and the two girls burst into stifled laughter.

"You're ridiculous," Kate said.

"I bet Kyle is ridiculous," Ember retorted. "In b—"

"Okay," Kate said. "I think that's enough. Just drop me off at home and I'll take my car from there."

"Sure you don't want to take Kyle for a ride?" Marta asked.

Kate jerked her head. "Not in the slightest."

"What's going on?" Reed asked. "What are Ember and Marta talking about?"

Kate unmuted the phone and furiously gestured for them to be silent. "You really think I'd take them on our date?" she mustered all the scorn she could muster, but Reed merely laughed.

"Yes," he said. "And my guess is that they wanted to go indoor skydiving and you didn't want to drive alone."

Kate groaned. "When did you figure it out?"

"When you kept muting the phone," Reed said smugly. "You've never muted the phone before and I got suspicious, so I texted Brittney."

Kate burst into a laugh, drawing Ember and Marta's attention. "What did he say?" Marta hissed.

Kate put the phone on speaker. "Brittney betrayed us," she said.

"I don't even know who to trust anymore," Ember grumbled.

"Hey Reed!" Marta said brightly. "I hope you don't mind us tagging along."

"Not at all," Reed said, the smile evident in his voice. "But I do want to hear what's going on with Kyle."

"Who?" Marta asked, glancing at Ember in surprise.

Kate's phone pinged and a picture appeared, the one Ember had surreptitiously taken when Kyle had stood outside her jeep. Kate's eyes flew to Ember but her expression had turned to one of horror.

"*Brittney*," she snapped the name like a curse.

"You sent a picture to Brittney?" Marta asked.

"How would I know she'd give it to Reed?" she growled.

"Don't feel bad," Reed said. "But I do think the world is already full of Hannah's, don't you think?"

Ember glared at Kate but she shook her head. Then she began to laugh when she noticed Marta's guilty expression. Ember stabbed a finger at her and she raised her hands defensively, trying to forestall Ember's impending outburst.

"You told Brittney our plan?"

"I saw you text the picture," Marta said. "I didn't think she'd tell Reed."

Kate enjoyed the image of Ember seething for a moment and then shifted so she could see her in the mirror. "I would have told him if Brittney didn't."

"You take all the fun out of dating," Ember grumbled.

"I'll take that as a compliment," Reed said.

Marta shook her head in chagrin. She opened her mouth to speak but then thought better of it, and instead pulled out her phone and texted a quick message. An instant later Kate's phone pinged and she read the message.

Hannah or no Hannah, Reed is yours.

Kate smiled and nodded in gratitude. The conversation had served to highlight the idea that Reed was wholly invested in their relationship, and not even Hannah could break the bonds that bound them together. They pulled into their driveway and Kate got out.

"Enjoy the rest of your date," Ember said caustically.

"Enjoy dinner with Kyle," Kate said.

"We will," Marta said.

Kate took it off speakerphone and hopped in her own car. As she backed into the street she began to laugh, the sight of the angry Ember boiling into amusement. When it subsided she shook her head in admiration.

"They would have milked that for weeks," she said.

"After you told me, of course."

His tone was still amused but carried a trace of doubt. "I would have, honestly," she said. "but I have to admit, it was nice thinking of you being the jealous one."

Reed chuckled to himself and she heard the clang of a door in the background. Prior to leaving Denver she'd directed him to a Panera Bread that was on the way back into Manhattan. As someone called out for the next person in line, Kate pulled into the Panera that was around the corner from her house.

"Are you really jealous?" Reed asked.

Kate considered the answer as she locked the door and entered the building. "Not of Hannah exactly," she said, "but of her time with you."

She hesitated and then added, "and I'm still concerned you could fall for her."

Reed's laugh made it sound absurd. "That's about as likely as you going out with Kyle."

It was Kate's turn to laugh. "Well played, Reed. Well played."

"I have my moments," he said. "Ready for dinner?"

"Starving," she replied.

They ordered and sat down to eat together. As she sipped her lemonade it occurred to her that her worries regarding Hannah rose and fell like the tide, occasionally threatening to overwhelm her, but other times it was a distant concern. She hoped that as more time passed it would leave her more frequently, and she could imagine a future with Reed after his internship.

". . . New York is so *expensive*," Reed was saying. "I don't know how anyone manages to live here."

"How are you doing on money?" she asked.

"Low," he admitted. "For an internship the institute pays well—but in New York it doesn't go very far. If I didn't have free rent I'd be on the street."

"You also spent all your money on my date to New York," she replied.

"That too," he said. "Which means our date next week will have to be on the conservative side."

"But it's our anniversary," she protested. "And Valentine's Day."

"I know," he said. "But I can't afford much."

"We've done plenty of inexpensive dates," she said. "I'm sure we can figure something out."

As they ate they talked about New York and Boulder, a topic in which Reed seemed very interested. Kate shared the details of what was going on with her roommates, and Jackson and Shelby, which were deep into planning their wedding.

"That explains why I don't get to talk to him often," Reed said. "He's been really busy lately."

"They want to get married in May," she said.

"That soon?" Reed asked, his surprise indicating he hadn't known. "I thought they'd decided to wait until the fall."

"Shelby's dad changed his mind," Kate said. "Turns out, he offered them an extra $5,000 for their wedding if they did it in May. Something to do with a business trip in the fall."

"That's manipulative," Reed said, his tone disapproving.

"That's what I said," Kate agreed. "But Jackson said he didn't care, and they might as well get the extra money."

"That's because they get to keep the extra," Reed said.

Kate paused in reaching for her bread. "What do you mean?"

"Shelby's dad said he'd give them $20,000—now $25,000—for the wedding, and anything leftover they got to keep. If they wanted to go over that, they'd have to pay for it themselves."

"Wow," Kate said, wondering what she'd do with the extra money. "I think I would have ended up with a lot."

"Me too," Reed said. "But last I heard, Shelby wants more extravagance than I would have thought."

"Every girl has their wedding fantasies," she said.

"Even you?" Reed asked.

"Even me," Kate said. She wondered if he'd steered the conversation on purpose, but didn't dare ask.

"I don't think you're a destination wedding type of girl," Reed mused. "No Tahiti or Hawaii."

"True," she said. "But I still want to go to Hawaii. Perhaps the honeymoon?"

"Maybe," Reed said, "But not a big wedding either. I suspect you'd want family and friends, maybe a chocolate fountain."

"With a white dress?" she shook her head. "Not a chance."

"So where would you want to get married?"

"I don't know," she said, shrugging, even though he couldn't see it. "I know what I don't want. No wedding on the beach or in the mountains, nothing crazy like skydiving. Maybe I'll know when I figure out who'll be at the end of the aisle." She couldn't resist the smile.

"I'll help you figure it out," he assured her.

"Don't tease a girl about a wedding," Kate warned with a laugh. "Not unless you have a plan to back it up."

"Point taken," he said. "But you never said what's going on with Ember and Tanner."

The shift in conversation was obviously intentional, but Kate wondered about the topic throughout their dinner. It could have been superficial, a casual talk about marriage between a couple—if that was possible—but she sensed a deeper question. Like an army sending out a scouting party. The topic had served to establish their expectations, and she hoped it meant he was legitimately considering the option.

They finished eating and caught a movie together, she in her theater, he in his. With their earpieces back on she could hear his movie, which was five minutes before hers. She sat alone but did not feel alone, and munched on her popcorn as he munched on his.

After the movie, Kate took Reed to get frozen custard. It had taken hours of research to find a location that was in New York close enough to Reed, and also in Boulder, but she'd managed to locate a chain they could both visit. With her cup in hand, she retreated to her car, shivering at the icy air.

"Would you want to live in New York after your doctorate?" Kate asked. She realized it was the first time she'd looked beyond the internship and enjoyed the image of the two of them together.

"Maybe," he said. "But not alone."

"Perhaps Hannah would like to be your roommate," Kate said.

She smiled, pleased that the statement held no rancor. "Maybe," Reed replied. "But I think the vacancy has already been filled."

"Reed Thompson," Kate said, feigning shock. "We haven't even slept together and you want me to move in with you?"

"Maybe," he said. "But if you did move here, we'd have to get a one bedroom apartment . . ."

He let the implication hang and Kate choked on the custard she'd just eaten. She sipped her water in a vain effort to cool off and then her eyes narrowed. "You know exactly what you're doing to me, don't you."

"Doesn't mean it's not true," he said.

She stirred her dessert and wondered if he was doing the same with his. "You know, we haven't really talked much about the future. What do you want beyond the internship?"

"My top four choices are Stanford, Harvard, Yale, and Princeton."

"And which is your favorite?"

"I think that depends on a few things," Reed said. "Namely, where would you want to go?"

It was the first time he'd outright said he wanted to be with her after the internship, and the prospect sent her heart fluttering. She put her bowl down before it could spill all over her shirt.

"I do finish in December," she said. "And Stanford has a good master's program."

As she spoke it aloud, it seemed the earth shifted, the stars aligning with a plan that had just been suggested, but rang with certainty. She took a breath to steady her thudding heart and reminded herself that there was a world of time between February and December.

"I find Stanford is suddenly at the top of my list," Reed said.

"It appears we have a plan," she said.

The thrill was sharp and poignant. They were already close, but it felt like they'd inched even closer, the gap between them narrowing like the day they'd first kissed. She sat back in her seat and realized she hadn't been worried about Hannah for hours. For the first time since Reed had left Boulder, she looked to the future.

And dared to hope.

Chapter 5

"How was your date?" Hannah asked when Reed arrived at the brownstone.

"Great," Reed said, glancing at the clock on the wall. He hadn't realized it was after eleven. "Where are Clint and David?"

"Still out," she said. "I think they wanted to hit a club."

Reed imagined the two interns, both going bald and both with glasses, at a club. They'd gone a couple of times since Reed had arrived, and he'd never have thought they would enjoy it, particularly David, who seemed quieter than Clint.

"And you didn't go?" Reed asked.

"Not really my scene anymore," Hannah said.

Feeling confident after his date with Kate, he collected two water bottles from the fridge and sank into the couch across from Hannah, who sat at the desk in the library. He tossed one to her and she caught it with a nod of gratitude.

"You're studying on a Friday night?"

"Actually looking at graduate programs," she said, turning her laptop to show him the screen. "My internship ends in July, so I need to finalize my applications for the fall semester. Dr. Pravesh and Dr. Dickson have written letters of recommendation, so I'm just going through the essay process."

Her grimace made Reed smile. "No one likes writing the essays."

She raised her bottle of water to his statement and then took a drink. "The college entrance essays are all the same. What makes you want to be a psychiatrist? What makes you think you're qualified for our program? What's a moment from your life that helped to define you?" She shook her head. "At least I have plenty of material."

The trace of bitterness on her features prompted Reed to frown. "Why *do* you want to be a psychiatrist?"

Hannah regarded him for several moments, her brown eyes unflinching as if she measured Reed's character. He wanted to keep his distance from Hannah, but the girl obviously needed someone to talk to, and there was no else.

"My parents got divorced when I was ten," Hannah said slowly. "My mom's second husband was abusive, and she divorced him two years later."

She said it dismissively, as if it didn't matter, but a darkness tinged her gaze. As if she knew Reed could see she it, she looked away, and only looked back when it was gone. Her smile hid what had appeared before, the flawless façade able to hide the truth from anyone else. But not Reed. He'd seen that look before, and knew what she didn't say.

Her mother wasn't the only one he'd abused.

"I'm sorry," Reed said.

Hannah shrugged. "I want to counsel women in abusive relationships—and help them get out."

"An admirable goal," Reed said. "And there's unfortunately plenty of women in that situation."

"Too true," Hannah said. "But it's nice to know there are a few good people out there."

Her eyes settled on Reed and a faint smile appeared before she shut her laptop and stood. Stretching and yawning, she changed the subject and then ascended the steps to her room. Alone, Reed sipped his water, wondering what had just happened.

The following day was Saturday, and Reed half expected Hannah to act differently, but she made no mention of their conversation the previous night. At first he thought the revelation had been intentional, another effort to bond them together, but as Reed spent the day with his roommates he realized she'd actually opened up.

He guessed it was just a moment of vulnerability when he happened to be present, and he pondered the ramifications of the information she'd shared—and not shared. As much as he wanted to keep his distance, he felt a desire to heal the harm that had been done to her.

Much of Sunday was spent holed up in the library, reviewing and writing papers and also planning their research for the week. David and Clint woke close to noon after spending Saturday night at another club, both with hangovers from the previous night's festivities.

As was rapidly becoming his custom, Reed stole time with Kate where he could, and spoke to her throughout the day. He chose not to share what Hannah had said, not because he didn't trust Kate, but because it was not his secret to share.

Monday morning dawned and the four interns arrived at the office in a cab together. The weather had grown cold enough over the weekend that they couldn't walk without arriving frostbitten. They walked inside as Reed and Hannah spoke of their upcoming pseudo-date. As Reed scribbled down a few notes for his and Hannah's excursion, Dr. Dickson called his name.

"Reed," he said, appearing in his office door. "Before you and Hannah go out, I'd like you to do me a favor."

Reed and Hannah exchanged a look. "I'll be in my office," Hannah said, and left.

Reed strode to Dr. Dickson's door and he motioned to the girl rising from the chair. She smiled as she caught sight of Reed and he wondered why she looked so familiar. The he blinked in recognition.

"Elaina?" he asked.

"I'm glad you remember my niece," Dr. Dickson said.

Dr. Dickson's niece had traded in the regal ball gown she'd worn at the benefit last week and now wore professional business attire.

Reed offered his hand. "It's good to see you again. What can I do for you?"

"Nothing," she said, glancing to her uncle. "I'm fine."

Dr. Dickson ignored her comment. "Elaina was just talking about how her boyfriend has been distracted of late, and I figured it was time for one of my interns to get a chance for real counseling. The Breakfast Nook around the corner should serve your purposes well, unless you have another location in mind."

Elaina's eyebrows knit together in a frown. "I need to apologize for my uncle. He likes to interfere."

"Just doing your father's duty," he said with an airy wave of his hand. "You two enjoy your morning." He then glanced at his watch. "I believe I have an emergency session to attend to." His eyes sparkling, he ushered them out and shut the door.

Reed exchanged an amused look with Elaina. "I guess brunch is in order?"

"I guess," she said with an annoyed sigh. "But don't expect me to share anything."

"I won't," Reed replied.

He walked to the elevator, pausing at Hannah's office to let her know he was going to brunch with Elaina. She said she would meet him after. When the elevator doors shut Elaina threw him a long look, and Reed smiled.

"Do all therapists receive such scrutiny?"

"Just wondering how it's going with Hannah."

He shrugged. "Fine. We work together."

"And live together," she said. "And get paid to date." He raised his eyebrow, surprised to hear that she knew about his research project.

Seeing his expression, she smiled faintly. "My uncle may not be my father, but he does tell me a few things."

"Hannah is just a friend," he said.

Her eyes narrowed. "A moment ago you said coworker."

He laughed and motioned to her. "Is this what it's like when two psychiatrists hang out? We both can't stop analyzing each other?"

"Maybe," she allowed. "But I'm not a doctor yet so I wouldn't know."

"She's a coworker and a friend," Reed said.

"Nothing more?"

"I have a girlfriend," he said. "One that I happen to be in love with."

The elevator dinged and they walked outside, both shivering at the blast of frigid air. As they strolled down the street Elaina shivered in the cold and he wondered if she would change the subject.

"I didn't realize you were with someone," she said. "How long have you been together?"

"A year," Reed said, and briefly told her about Kate.

"My boyfriend is Warren," she said, and then grimaced. "Well done establishing a rapport. Now I feel the need to share."

Reed grinned. "Once a shrink, always a shrink."

She laughed and consented with a nod. "Warren is the son of an investment banker—one who owns a third of the firm. He has more money than he knows what to do with."

"How did you meet him?"

"Our mothers wanted us to go out," she said. "And I did like him, at first. Around his family he was the model son, but when he's with me he becomes crass and rebellious, everything my mom would not approve of."

"Are you dating a bad boy?" he asked, feigning shock.

She grinned and motioned to him. "You know, you have my uncle's sense of humor. He has this way of making everyone smile and they just want to spill all their secrets. It's actually rather irritating."

"Did you indirectly call me irritating?"

Her smile widened and she shook her head. "See? Irritating." Then she sighed and looked away. "And I'm deflecting."

"Why don't you tell me what's going on now?"

She was silent for several moments and he guessed she was deciding whether or not to talk. When she described Warren, Reed had gotten the idea she kept the truth from Dr. Dickson—a truth he'd probably guessed at, which explained why he'd sent Reed in his stead.

"At first it was fun," Elaina said, evidently deciding to share. "We'd do things I would never have done on my own. But lately he's pushing it further than I'd like, and last week he showed up at my apartment with cocaine."

"Don't you live in the city?" Reed asked, using the softer question to keep her talking.

She motioned vaguely north. "A few blocks up from here, actually. I live with my mother—who would go ballistic if she knew."

"And you're studying addiction recovery," he said.

"I was tempted," she admitted. "And I didn't expect that. I've never done drugs, but I wanted to see what it was about. Fortunately my mom arrived and he bolted."

"When was all this?"

"Friday."

"Ah," Reed said. "Which is why you visited Dr. Dickson today."

"I asked him for advice on a client at my internship," she said. "But I think he guessed the truth. Then he spotted you and called you in."

"And you decided to tell me everything."

She laughed. "Most of it, probably because you aren't connected to my family or friends—who all know Warren. Our mothers even sit on the board for the same charity."

"Can I see your phone?"

"Why?" she asked, but removed it and handed it him.

It was unlocked, so Reed scrolled through favorites on the contact list and found Warren's name. Pulling it up, he typed a quick text. Elaina craned her head to see what he was writing and her eyes widened. She reached for the phone.

"You can't send that."

"I'm not going to," Reed said. He handed the phone to her. "We both know what you want to do. If you hit send, you know you want to end things. If you delete, you know your feelings run deeper."

She stared at the words he'd typed that would end her relationship. He'd kept it brief but firm. Normally he would never have suggested breaking up via text, but Warren sounded manipulative and controlling, and if she tried to break up in person he might talk her out of it. She lifted her thumb . . . and pressed the button to send.

"Feel better?" Reed asked.

They came to a stop in front of The Breakfast Nook, which served artisanal breakfast throughout the day. She shook her head and looked him up and down like she was just seeing him.

"You helped me fix my problem on a walk to brunch," she said, her tone tinged with admiration. "I can see why my uncle likes you."

Reed shrugged. "He's the expert," he said. "But we might as well grab brunch while we're here."

Elaina caught his arm as he turned away. "You helped me so I'll help you. Watch out for Hannah. She puts on a nice show, but she knows what she wants, and knows how to get it."

"I'll be careful," Reed said, and thought of what Hannah had shared.

"And don't tell my uncle about Warren," she said.

Reed grinned and held the door for her. "Doctor patient confidentiality."

She laughed lightly and walked past him, and a moment later they talked about her now ex-boyfriend's return text. Elaina was nice, clever, and driven, and he sensed a true friendship in the making. She respected him, but was not attracted to him, and he fleetingly wished she and Hannah had traded spots. It certainly would have made his life easier.

Chapter 6

"How is Elaina?" Hannah asked as they climbed into the cab.

"Good," Reed said. "Dr. Dickson just thought I could help her with something."

"What about?"

The question was mild but Reed heard what she really meant. *Is she a threat?* Reed smiled, perversely pleased that Hannah was a shade jealous of Elaina. Still, he had no desire to further thoughts that could cause problems in the future.

"Nothing big," he replied with a shrug. "But I like her. She reminds me of my sister."

Hannah relaxed, the difference nearly imperceptible, but noticeable because he was paying attention. She nodded as if the answer was expected and then leaned down to examine her tablet, which showed the document they'd spent the weekend crafting.

"Ready for a real date?" she asked.

"Ready for a fake date," Reed corrected.

"We're supposed to pretend this is real," Hannah countered.

"Just as long you remember it's not," he said with a faint smile.

She flashed a coy smile and pointed south. "First up, Coney Island."

"Do you still think it should be on the list?"

"I do," she said. "You were right. People come from out of town to go to Coney Island, especially in families. The wealthier socialites don't go there."

"Not very often," the cab driver called back.

Reed agreed with their point. "Which is what makes this perfect. The couple that will be going on this date have been together for ten years, but the information we have is that he works all the time and she rarely goes out. They both need excitement and a date like this will remind them of their dating years, hopefully rekindling their attraction for each other."

"The Ten Kisses Date," she said.

He nodded in approval at the title. "We just need the locations."

"Try the Ferris wheel," the cab driver suggested.

"Already on the list," Hannah said.

Obviously wanting to be part of the conversation, the driver continued to offer suggestions all the way to Coney Island. When they got out both Reed and Hannah laughed. As they turned to the entrance Hannah motioned to the driver.

"I think *he* wants to go on this date."

"I think most anyone that's single wants to go on a date," Reed said.

Hannah arched an eyebrow. "I hadn't thought of it that way."

"Think about it," Reed said. "In your first few years of college, how many nights did you and your roommates talk about how much you wished guys would ask you out?"

"It's disturbing how much you know us," Hannah said.

"Doesn't take a genius to figure it out," Reed replied with a shrug. "Girl's want what guys are afraid to give."

"And what's that?"

"Time," Reed said simply.

She chuckled dryly. "All too true—except for the ones that get clingy and want to give so much time they smother the girl."

As they talked, they threaded their way through the crowd. It was a cold Monday morning without a holiday, so the crowd was sparse. Roller coasters, large tents, and other attractions lined the boardwalk, interspersed with shops and places to eat. Clowns, acrobats, and magicians performed on the street, giving the island a carnival air. Known for its coney dogs, the island had an abundance of hot dog restaurants, with each claiming specific variations of the famous treat.

Reed and Hannah set out to explore the park, their goal to find ten locations the Youngs would have to find. Once located, the couple were to take a picture and then kiss before crossing it off the list.

"They can't be too hard to find or they'll get frustrated," Hannah said.

"But not too easy either," Reed said.

Several were easy to pick, like the top of the Ferris wheel, the front cart of the roller coaster, and a statue. From there it got more difficult, forcing them to explore the entire island in search of great places.

"The board by the beach," Hannah said, adding it to the list. "That's seven."

Reed pulled out his phone and texted Kate the selfie he'd taken at the beach, smiling when the response came quickly. Hannah had offered to take the picture for him but he'd declined, not wanting Kate to have a reminder that she was with him.

They took a break for lunch and ate at Nathan's Famous, adding it to the list and agreeing it was famous for a reason. The frigid air had driven many inside, and the restaurant was full, forcing Hannah to sit close to him in a small booth. He tried not to let his discomfort show on his face.

"I can feel my heart stopping," Reed said, picking up a fry smothered in bacon and cheese, "but I love it."

"Everyone says cholesterol is bad for you," Hannah said. "But it certainly makes food delicious."

Reed wiped his hands on a napkin and picked up the list. "Nathan's is last on the list," he said. "Why don't we review it and see if anything needs to be changed."

"Let's take a break from the Ten Kisses Date," she said. "What do you think about our plans for next week?"

"I like the idea of going to the Brooklyn Botanic Garden," Reed said.

"In March it will be cherry blossom season, so it should be beautiful," Hannah replied. Then she laughed to herself. "You know, you've already taken me on more dates than anyone else."

"That's a disturbing indictment of my gender," Reed said,

As they were cleaning up their food, Reed noticed a young couple nearby looking around, a camera in hand. Hannah noticed as well and offered to take their picture, which they gladly accepted. Hannah stepped back and snapped the photo.

"Can you take one of us?" she asked.

Reed blinked in surprise but the woman was already standing. "Of course," she said, accepting Hannah's phone. Then she spotted Reed and her eyes widened slightly. "You make a gorgeous couple," she said.

"We work together," Reed said, but Hannah spoke over him.

"Thank you, but we aren't together."

Hannah winked, and the girl smiled. Reed frowned, but forced a smile when the woman raised the phone and Hannah scooted closer. Reed wanted to lean away but felt trapped, and was grateful when the woman lowered the phone.

"One more," Hannah said, "Just in case."

"Of course," the woman said.

Stiff and irritated, Reed managed a smile for the woman's sake. Hannah seemed not to notice his rigid posture and leaned even closer, pressing her curvy body against his and letting her dark hair fall down his shoulder. Just as the picture snapped Hannah turned.

And planted a kiss on his cheek.

Her lips were soft and sent energy coursing into his body, but it wasn't pleasant. Reed flinched away but the woman laughed and handed the phone back to Hannah, who smiled in gratitude.

"Thank you."

"You're welcome," the woman said, and smirked as she strode away.

Reed waited until she was gone before turning on Hannah. "What do you think you're doing?"

"Just playing the role," Hannah said, shrugging nonchalantly. "But she's right, we make a cute couple."

"*Hannah*," he said, lowering his voice so others wouldn't hear his anger. "That was not okay."

"It's just a kiss on the cheek," Hannah said with a dismissive wave. "It's not like we slept together."

"It doesn't matter," Reed said. "I know what you feel about me but you can't cross lines like that."

A flicker of anger crossed her features and she stood. "Don't pretend you're not attracted to me."

She picked up the wrappers from the meal and walked away, dropping them in the trash can on the way out. Reed stood and followed her, his long stride allowing him to catch her outside the restaurant.

"I'm not attracted to you," Reed said.

She folded her arms, pressing her chest upward. "I know I'm attractive, and we spend every morning going on dates. You can't deny all this time together doesn't mean anything to you."

"We do this for *work*," Reed said. "And you are attractive. But I'm in love with Kate, and that's not going to change. You need to understand that. You need to *accept* that."

"You can't deny we have a connection," she said, stabbing a finger at him. "We plan these dates and we think alike. The way we feel about romance is the same—and not just because we're planning it for other couples. You may love Kate, but right now you're with me."

"I'm not *with* you," Reed said. "We may have to work together tomorrow, but right now, we aren't friends, we aren't coworkers, we aren't anything."

Her features darkened. "You can't stop talking to me. We live in the same house—and we work together."

"That can change," he warned.

"You'd give up on your dreams to get away from me?" she scoffed. "I don't believe you. Do you have any idea how many guys would give their right arm to be with me? Just for one night."

"I'm not one of them," Reed said. "And I haven't even spent the night with Kate. What makes you think I'd do that with you?"

It was meant as a scathing insult, but Hannah's eyes widened in surprise and she gave him a measuring look. He suddenly realized how much she could read into the statement and sought to backtrack, but it was too late.

"You're a virgin," she said, the anger gone from her voice.

"If you must know, yes," he said.

"What was it? Religion? Personal commitment? Trauma?"

He didn't like the gleam of attraction that had blossomed in her eyes, so he turned and walked away with a parting, "I think this non-date just ended."

"Don't you see?" she asked, falling into step beside him. "This explains so much. If you loved her, you would have slept with her. And there's so much I can show you—"

"No," he said turning on her. She retreated from the heat in his tone and he lowered his voice, conscious of the people walking nearby. "No," he repeated. "You're not going to show me anything, because it's not you I want to be with."

"Every straight guy wants to see a girl naked—wants to see *me* naked."

He looked at her with pity in his eyes. "You really have no idea how to build a real relationship."

She flinched as if he'd struck a physical blow, and he used the moment to escape. "I think we should take separate rides home," he said.

He turned and walked away, and this time she did not follow. As he walked away he seethed about what Hannah had done, but some of the anger was directed at himself, and he struggled to identify where he'd given Hannah the idea that she had a chance. He found a taxi and gave the address of the institute, the streets blurring by as he fought his anger. His phone buzzed and he expected Hannah or Kate, but instead it was Jackson. Reed frowned as he read the message.

Dude, what did you do?

What? Reed responded.

Look at Ember's blog, Jackson said.

Reed felt a sinking feeling as he used his phone to look up Ember's blog. Following the links to the latest post, he froze when he found the picture of him and Hannah, her lips squarely on his cheek.

Chapter 7

Kate checked her phone for the hundredth time that day, wishing Reed had texted. He usually found time to text her during the mornings he was with Hannah, a fact Kate appreciated. Kate guessed it was because Reed missed her most when he had to be on one of their pseudo dates.

She listened to her roommates talk as Marta drove them to the north side of campus. Her mind in New York, she didn't hear Ember call her name until she raised her voice. Then Kate looked up and saw Ember's annoyed expression.

"Today's about Shelby, remember?"

Kate nodded and shook herself. "I'm sorry," she said, and meant it.

Shelby had waited months for today, and Kate wasn't about to spoil it with her missing Reed. Shaking herself, she tuned into the conversation as Marta pulled into the parking lot and looked for a spot.

"When did Shelby's mom get in?" Brittney asked.

"Yesterday," Ember said.

"I can't believe she's letting us help her pick a dress," Brittney said, excited. "I've never done this before."

"Me either," Kate said.

"I've helped a few cousins," Marta said. "And they all came here for their dresses."

"It's nice of Alanis to give Shelby a discount," Brittney said.

Kate had met Alanis a few times and privately disliked the girl. She was one of Marta's many cousins in town, but Kate had found her to be too shallow for them to really be friends. Perhaps that's why she worked a bridal shop.

They parked and got out, passing Shelby's car on the way to the door. Boulder Bridal sat next to the eastern campus in Boulder and was popular for college students needing formal wear. It was Kate's first time inside the store, and she looked around in interest.

Dresses were displayed in the window to the right, while accessories hung on racks to the left. A counter sat in front while other displays ringed the room. Racks of tuxes and dresses were prominently visible. Shelby stood with her mom behind the counter, and turned when the door swung open. She smiled and waved them over.

"Mom," Shelby said. "This is Kate, Ember, Brittney, and Marta."

"Call me Idra," she said, greeting them.

Idra looked a lot like Shelby, her blond hair highlighted with a few strands of silver, her smile easy and often. But Idra was as short as Ember and on the plump side, indicating Shelby had gotten her athletic build from her father.

"Is your party ready?" A woman asked, approaching the group.

"Let's find me a dress," Shelby said with a nervous smile.

The group scattered to the racks and displays, hunting like their lives depended on it. Kate browsed with Brittney, examining dresses made by a designer named Willowby. Although undeniably beautiful, Kate and Brittney looked at each other and shook their heads.

"She wanted one with different sleeves," Brittney said.

"What about this?" Idra asked, lifting a dress out by a designer named Maggie Sottero.

Long and flowing outward, the dress was the right size. Lace straps hung over the shoulders while a satin tie wrapped around the waist. Simple and elegant, it drew approval from all of them.

"Maggie is one of our most popular designers," the employee said, eyeing Shelby. "Would you like to try it on?"

Kate smiled at Shelby's obvious excitement, and the group followed the employee as she led them into the back room. A changing room was off to the side, while a pedestal faced a quartet of large mirrors. Idra and Shelby disappeared into the changing room and Kate took a seat in one of the chairs set around the room. Ember flopped into the chair next to her.

"Just being in this room makes me want to get married," Ember said.

"You and me both," Marta said, examining a dress on display. "Do you think we can try them on, even if we aren't getting married?"

"I don't think that's a good idea," Kate said, already wondering what it would be like to see Reed in a tux, in person. He'd sent her pictures from the benefit, but she wanted to see him in person, to run her hands up his back. "That will just make me want it more."

"Come on," Ember said. "You can't tell us you haven't thought about Reed and you getting married. You two are made for each other."

"He moves pretty slow," she hedged.

"That's true," Brittney said. "Thirteen dates to the kiss? A hundred dates to propose?"

They laughed together and Marta nodded. "Three years to go."

Kate grinned and endured their teasing. Privately she did wonder, and recalled the few times she'd allowed herself to imagine a life with Reed. It was a fantasy she didn't dare share with her roommates.

Shelby exited the changing room, her face flushed and nervous. For the normally confident woman, the expression was out of place, especially when she had no need to be self-conscious. The sight of her body draped in white drew them all their feet.

"What do you think?" she asked.

"Riveting," Kate said with a nod.

"Jackson's going to be speechless," Ember said.

"A first for him," Marta added.

Shelby grinned and took a breath before stepping onto the pedestal. Then she turned a circle, her expression shocked as she viewed herself in the elegant gown. It really did look incredible, framing her waist and her torso perfectly, accentuating the curves while showing just a hint of skin.

Kate suppressed the touch of envy that she assumed was just the natural part of visiting a bridal shop with a friend. But she did imagine herself standing on the pedestal, also draped in white . . .

"I can't breathe," Shelby said.

"That's normal before a wedding," Brittney said.

Shelby laughed. "No, I mean it's really tight. Is that normal?" She glanced to the employee.

"I'm not sure if we have a larger size in stock," the woman said.

The trace of condescension, as if the athletic Shelby was too large for the wedding dress, did not go unnoticed by the group. Ember bristled and rose to her feet as Marta put a hand on her arm to restrain her. Kate caught Ember's other hand, hoping she could keep Ember from mauling the woman. Then Idra stepped in.

"I'm sorry," she said sincerely. "I didn't realize this was a bridal shop for the tiny percentage of the population small enough to be considered perfect. Perhaps there is another store in Boulder that has dresses for everyone else?"

Her tone was not angry or forceful, and even sounded apologetic. But her features veritably dripped with animosity, causing the girl to flush. She nodded and departed, and a moment later a different girl returned with a different size.

She smiled warmly. "Perhaps this will be a better fit?"

Kate was sitting closest to the opening that led to the front of the store, and heard snippets of a hushed conversation between the manager and the first girl. The voices were quiet but the anger was real, and Kate got the impression the store did not support her opinion. She smiled, grateful that the good things they'd heard about Boulder Bridal were true.

"I like her," Ember said, motioning to Shelby's mom.

"You would," Kate said.

Ember smirked and then went to answer Marta. Shelby took a call from Jackson and laughed as she teased him about what she was wearing. Idra claimed a seat next to Kate and leaned over to her.

"I always knew she'd get married before my boys," she said. "But it's still hard to imagine her as a married woman."

"Shelby and Jackson are perfect for each other," Kate said, watching Shelby talk on the phone.

Idra turned to her, a small smile on her face. "I understand you are the one most likely to follow in my daughter's footsteps."

"You mean . . ." Kate motioned to the wedding dresses, and Idra nodded. Kate flushed. "I don't think so. Reed and I are still taking things slow."

"*Glacier* slow," Brittney said, looking up from a bridal magazine. She gave Kate a meaningful look.

Kate flushed again, uncomfortable with the turn in the conversation. "Don't look at me like that. I'm happy where I am."

Ember issued a grunt that expressed a world of doubt. Kate glared at her but she shrugged and pulled out her phone. Then Idra patted Kate on the knee.

"Shelby has shown me your friend's blog," Idra said. "I even learned a few things, and asked my husband on a date."

"Really?" Kate asked.

Idra smiled. "We went line dancing. My husband may be a nerd, but he's got more rhythm that I expected."

"Sounds like a great night," Kate said.

"It was," she said. "And the long drive made it even better."

"Drive?" Brittney asked.

"We drove to Texas for the weekend," she admitted.

"All to go to a dance hall?" Kate asked.

"It was the one I wanted to go to when I was in high school," she said, "but I was never asked. Going on a date with my husband was an entirely different experience."

"Someday I hope to do that," Kate said.

"Is it serious?" Idra asked.

"Yes," Ember said, and then leaned over and lowered her voice. "But she hasn't even had sex with him yet."

"*Ember*," Kate said.

Ember shrugged and returned her attention to her phone. "It's true."

"My husband was a virgin when we got married," Idra said. "It may be an archaic notion, but I like being the only one he's ever slept with."

"*Mom*," Shelby groaned. "I really don't want to hear about you and dad . . ." She cringed.

Idra patted Kate on the knee and winked. "You may want to start looking for your own dress."

Kate managed to keep the smile from her face, unwilling to reveal that was exactly what she'd been thinking about. The next moment Shelby finished talking to Jackson and disappeared into the changing room to try another dress.

For the next hour Shelby donned and discarded several worthy competitors. Kate browsed the dresses on the racks, doing her best not to imagine a wedding with Reed, and utterly failing. Brittney brought her a magazine depicting a wedding in a sunlit grove, and they laughed about what they would choose in their own futures.

As they talked weddings, Kate endured the lingering looks from her friends. She suspected that if the moment wasn't dedicated to Shelby, they would be bombarding her with questions. Privately, Kate thought about what a wedding would be like with Reed, of him in a tux while she walked down the aisle, the easy smile she'd come to love flashing across his face. With sunlight cascading through bright windows and dancing off white flowers, the image was perfect, and she found a yearning in her soul for such a future. When no one was looking, she dared to hope, a tentative smile on her lips . . .

Ember swore, the sound so harsh that everyone turned. Shelby, in her dress, looked back at herself in concern, her expression alarmed, as if she was worried she'd accidently torn the dress. Then she saw Ember's expression.

"What happened?" she asked.

Ember's eyes flicked to Kate, the single glance enough for dread to pool in Kate's belly. It had to do with her, but Ember's features were not the usual anger. Instead it was almost pain in her eyes, pain for Kate.

"What?" Kate asked.

Marta leaned over to see Ember's phone and her eyes went wide. "It's probably nothing," Marta said.

"What?" Kate asked, an edge creeping into her voice.

Ember grimaced. "Look on my blog."

Kate fumbled for her phone as she fought to quell her mounting dread. Her phone came on slowly and she felt the eyes of those in the room, the weight causing her stomach to clench. Then she turning on the web browser and navigated to Ember's blog, to see the last picture that had been posted.

Of Hannah kissing Reed.

Chapter 8

Kate stared at the phone, the images of her future disappearing as if the dresses had pulled themselves from the racks and flitted away. Someone called her name but she didn't hear, the image on the screen searing into her consciousness.

They were at a restaurant, a half-finished meal between them. Reed wore a snug thermal shirt that hugged his upper body, while Hannah wore a cleavage-baring shirt and a sleek leather jacket. Her dark hair touched his shoulder, while her lips brushed his cheek. But it was his smile that crushed her soul.

"Kate," Marta said. "I'm sure it was just a stunt or something."

"She's sitting really close for a stunt," Brittney said.

"If it's not a stunt, I'll kill him," Ember said, folding her arms. "I'll get my handgun from my jeep, drive up to his house and—"

Abruptly conscious that they were ruining Shelby's day, Kate retreated. "I'm sorry, Shelby," she mumbled. "I'll be outside."

Shelby raised a hand. "Wait—"

But Kate was already out the door. She walked down the sidewalk, trying not to think, to feel. All the fear she'd had about Hannah rose up like a tidal wave, threatening to drag her into its depths. Her phone buzzed and she realized it was still in her hand. Then she saw who it was.

Anger sparked but it could not overpower the numbness. Lifting the phone, she answered with a quiet, "Hey."

He must have heard it in her voice, because he growled. "I'm sorry, Kate, but it's not what you think. She cornered me and took advantage of the moment."

"She kissed you, Reed," Kate said, her voice wooden. "For you that's like a night in a hotel."

"It's not like that," he said. "She was taking a picture for someone else and then they were taking a picture of us—"

"While you were on your date."

Anger crept into her numb tone but she didn't fight the surge of strength. She needed it, because it pushed away the pain, pushed the image away from her consciousness. But it had its own strength, and remained fixed in her mind.

"It wasn't a date," he said, sounding like he was rubbing his forehead. "You know that. It was just work."

"Maybe I don't know that anymore," she said, her voice rising. "I warned you about Hannah and you didn't listen."

"What did you want me to do?" he asked. "Give up on my career because a girl was interested in me?"

"She was dangerous and I knew it," Kate said.

"I can't choose my life based on who happens to like me," he said.

"Yet that's exactly what you did with me," she said.

She knew it was an irrational thing to say but she couldn't seem to get the budding fury to form into the right words. Reed had betrayed everything, sacrificed what they had because he wouldn't listen. He should have listened.

"Kate," he said softly.

Tears formed in her eyes but she fought them back. "Don't," she said. "You let her *kiss* you, Reed. You let her get close to you."

"I should have listened to you," he said.

59

Her anger surged, because Reed was merely agreeing in an effort to placate her, not because he thought he was wrong. Her fingers hurt and she looked down, suddenly realizing her hand was balled so tightly her fingernails had dug into her palm.

"Don't patronize me," Kate said evenly. "I'm not stupid. We both know you protected yourself because you're smart. But she still managed to get close. And you couldn't stop her."

"I'll be more careful."

"It won't matter," she said. "She's already corrupting you, and you don't even see it."

He was silent for several moments and she stood, the anger boiling in her, threatening to spill out like a bomb. When he did speak his voice was also angry, but controlled, like he didn't want their words to escalate.

"I do see her attempts," he said. "Every time. I watch for them, I avoid them, I make sure every time we are alone at the Brownstone that I do not sit next to her. When we are at work I make sure we walk apart from each other—even in a cab I keep space between us. I think about it all the time."

"So you *are* thinking about her all the time."

He groaned. "Kate, listen to yourself. I'm careful because I'm thinking of *you*."

"Were you thinking of me when she kissed you?"

"It was just on the cheek," he said.

"It's not this kiss that I'm afraid of," Kate almost exploded. "It's the next, and the one after that. You're in New York and I'm here. I can't compete with that."

"You don't have to compete with anything," Reed said. "You've already won."

"Apparently I haven't."

"Will you stop talking like this?" Reed said. "I didn't cheat on you."

"You never would," Kate said, the anger spilling into hot tears. "But you would break up with me to be with her."

"Hannah doesn't mean anything to me," Reed said, his voice also angry. "What will it take for you to trust me?"

"I *did* trust you," she said. "Until I saw a picture of her kissing you."

"I can't prove to you that I'm loyal," he snapped. "I'm doing the best I can but it never feels like enough. A girl kissed me on the cheek, taking advantage of the moment. And do you know what I did next? I walked out, almost yelled at her, and then took my own cab home."

"You would never have let her get that close if we were married," she retorted.

She regretted it as soon as the word left her mouth, because it showed what she'd been considering. Revealing such a hope when they were close would have been hard enough, but doing it now was unthinkable.

"What do you want from me?" Reed asked. "Because maybe I can't be what you want."

"I wanted you," she said, all the anger abruptly draining form her voice. "But you chose New York."

It was a low blow and she knew it. They had chosen it together, because there hadn't been a better option. But in that moment she didn't care. Reed had left, and now her worst fears were being confirmed. Hannah was getting closer, while Kate and Reed were drifting apart.

"Maybe it's best we talk later," Reed said rigidly. "Before we say things we're going to regret."

"You already kissed her," she said. "Not much more you could do unless you climbed into her—"

"Kate," he snapped. "Stop. I'm sorry. I truly am. But you have to decide if you can forgive me."

She wanted to forgive him, but the image of Hannah draped on his body returned to her thoughts, bringing with it a stabbing pain. Losing Reed now would be agony, but it would be nothing compared to what she would endure if Reed ended things later. He was the best guy she had ever known, and if things ended like that, she would be alone forever.

"Maybe we should take some time to think things through," she said quietly.

"What are you saying?" Reed asked.

"Maybe we shouldn't talk for a while," she said, fighting the anger and regret that seemed to be battling for her soul.

She expected him to argue, to fight for her, and a flicker of hope pierced the roiling emotions in her chest. But after a moment of silence he spoke a single word, crushing her anew.

"Fine," he said, his voice hard. "If that's what you want."

She wanted to scream, *That's not what I want!* Instead her voice was just as hard. "I'll talk to you later, Reed."

"Bye, Kate."

There was a click on the phone, the sound conveying such a note of finality that she flinched. She lowered her phone and stared at the screen, and the words she'd seen a thousand times and never really noticed.

Call Ended.

Numb, she turned and walked to Ember's jeep. It wasn't until she was a few feet away that she realized all three of her roommates were there, as was Shelby. Ignoring their halting questions, Kate opened the door and got in.

After a hissed conversation, they got in as well, even Shelby, and they drove home in silence. Many meaningful looks were shared, but even Ember remained silent. Only when they pulled in did Kate notice the receipt in Shelby's hand, and realized she'd found her wedding dress.

"Congratulations, Shelby," she said, grateful her voice did not tremble. "I know you'll be happy with Jackson."

"Thanks," Shelby said, her expression worried. "Everything okay with Reed?"

Kate tried to speak and failed. And tried again, and failed again. Then the tears came, flowing down her cheeks in embarrassing rivers. She sought to wipe them away but the effort was futile.

Someone shoved a napkin into her hands and the kind gesture shattered what remained of her restraint. She was highly conscious of the cold seat and the warm air blowing in her hair, of her feet on the floor, and the seat belt across her chest, digging into her shoulder.

"What happened?" Ember finally demanded.

"I ended it," Kate whispered. "It's over."

She turned and stared out the window, the tears coming in silent waves. The girls began to talk, their voices a flood of indecipherable sound. While in the wedding store she'd imagined a bright future, but that had crumbled in an instant. What hurt the most was the desire to call Reed, and the fear he would not answer the phone. That he would never answer again.

Chapter 9

For three days Reed went to work and back to the brownstone, the days blurring into a stream of inconsequential faces. He spoke like everything was normal, the façade lasting until he shut his bedroom door at the end of the night. Then he pulled out his phone for the hundredth time and stared at the list of messages that had not been returned.

You know I would never cheat on you.

Kate, please call me.

I miss you.

I love you.

The silence from Kate felt like a scathing rebuke that settled in like a broken bone, the ache never diminishing, never out of mind. His efforts to hide were in vain, and the pack of psychiatrists all figured out what had happened the moment one of them thought to look at Ember's blog.

Ember had deleted the picture within an hour of Hannah posting it, but the comments were filled with arguments over the truth. Most seemed to think Kate could trust Reed, but there were plenty that thought Reed was just like any other guy, that he'd cheated within a month of leaving Kate in Boulder.

The divide was less pronounced at the institute, where the other interns, the doctors, and even the receptionist at the door blamed Hannah. It wasn't overt, but the receptionist was slow to open the elevator when Hannah forgot her passkey, and the other doctors assigned her extra papers.

Reed hardly noticed the unspoken support, his thoughts dominated by Kate, by what had happened, and how he could fix the fissure in their relationship. Dr. Dickson indirectly asked if he was able to continue the research project and Reed simply nodded.

"I intend to finish," he said.

Dr. Dickson gave him a searching look but ultimately agreed, and each morning Reed went out with Hannah to plan more dates. At all times he kept his distance, his conversation overly formal and professional. At first Hannah tried to act like everything was normal, but as each day passed her perpetual smile faded.

Two days before Valentine's Day, Reed finished his work late and left the office. The other interns had all left and most of the doctors, so he rode the elevator to the first floor alone. When they dinged open the receptionist stood.

"There's a letter for you, Reed."

"A letter?" Reed asked.

He accepted the note and frowned. The plain envelope contained no lettering except his name, which had been typed onto the front. He opened it and withdrew a simple note, also typewritten, that gave a time and a location. The Empire State Building.

His heart thumped in his chest like it was beating for the first time in days, the blood filling his body and sending warmth all the way to his fingers. It was impossible, and yet the *K* at the bottom revealed the sender.

"Reed?" the receptionist asked.

Reed looked up, shocked to find himself still standing in the lobby. "Sara," he said urgently. "Can you make sure my laptop gets back to my office?"

"Of course," she said, accepting the bag. "But what's so urgent . . .?"

Reed was already out the door. He whistled for a cab and one pulled in, the board above advertising roses and chocolates for Valentine's Day. He gave the destination and the cab pulled into traffic. Cars, buses, and trucks clogged the streets, slowing them almost to a crawl. Reed chaffed at the delay but spotted a flower shop ahead.

"Pull over up there, would you?" he asked.

He handed him a fifty and got out. Sprinting to the store, he rushed inside and grabbed a dozen roses before darting into line. Five minutes later he rushed outside and jumped back into the cab.

"Ready," he said.

"Looks like you've got a hot date," he said.

"That I do," he said.

He pulled out his phone but there was no message, and he typed out a question. Then he thought better of it and deleted the words, closing the app to fidget and watch the passing lights of the city. If Kate had used paper, then he didn't want to spoil her plans.

How had she done it? When did she buy her ticket? Why not just call him? The questions bombarded his mind and made him sweat, the cool air failing to alleviate the confusion and hope. When they got close the traffic came to a stop but he couldn't stand to wait. Throwing money into the front seat, he left the cab and sprinted down the sidewalk, dodging knots of people.

He raced four blocks to the Empire State Building and then to the ticket counter, where he was forced to wait as a family of six bought their tickets. When he stepped up he gave his name and the woman nodded.

"There's a VIP ticket waiting for you," she said.

Reed grinned, his elation soaring, and grabbed the ticket before heading to the front of the line and joining the next group in the elevator. The interminably long ride left him alone with his questions, and he again struggled to explain why Kate had come all this way.

The doors opened and he was the first one out. He rushed through the large room to the doors, his thoughts on the last time he'd stood on the building with Kate, just four weeks ago. He stepped into a blast of cold air and cast about, desperate to find Kate, to see her smile, to wrap her in his arms. Then a girl turned and he spotted her.

Hannah.

His elation burned to ash, leaving bitterness in his mouth. Without a word he turned and dropped the roses into the trash before striding towards the elevator. Hannah rushed to catch up and caught his arm. He pulled free.

"Please don't go," she said.

"I can't believe you would do this," Reed growled.

"I didn't know what to do," Hannah said. "You wouldn't talk to me—"

"And this will help?" Reed asked. Others looked his way and he lowered his voice. "You've taken what I value most in my life, and think that tricking me here will somehow make me fall for you?"

"I just want to talk to you," Hannah said. She closed the gap and tried to wrap her hands around Reed's waist, but he retreated. "I don't think you know how much I like you."

Her voice was soft, vulnerable, and he realized she was being sincere. For an instant he saw a life with her, of going on dates in New York, of going to school together, their research gaining renown, of them speaking at conferences. He saw their kids and their house. He saw their future.

But the image was tinged with regret, a loss that would tarnish their lives. Reed loved Kate, and that would not fade, not in a lifetime. All at once he saw Hannah for who she was, recognized all her actions, her intentions, her manipulations and vulnerability.

"Hannah," he said softly.

Mistaking his tone for consent, she glided forward with hope in her eyes, but Reed's next words brought her to a halt.

67

"You don't have feelings for me."

"I know what I feel," Hannah said.

"No," Reed said. "You don't. Every guy you've ever known, you got their attention using your body, your beauty. I think you saw me and realized you wanted more out of a relationship, so you used the same things that had worked so many times before. You're playing a game, but I'm not even on the field."

"You want a guy that will love you for more than your looks, and deep down you're afraid that will never happen. But you deserve a guy who will love you, not because you are beautiful, but because you are you."

Hannah stared at him, moisture gathering in her eyes. She tried to smile but failed, and then looked away. When she looked back her expression had hardened into anger, but even that was fleeting.

"You cannot imagine what I've been through."

"More than you'd think," he said, "and you have no idea how much I admire you. You've endured terrible things, but overcome them to build a career. You deserve respect—for your brain and your body. But you still doubt yourself. I saw it the night you told me what happened to your mom, the night of the benefit, and I see it right now. Despite all you've done, you still feel like you aren't okay unless you have a guy."

A tear trickled down Hannah's cheek and she wiped it away with the back of her hand. Reed had stripped away her confidence, her courage, her ambition, and laid bare her fear. Reed grimaced and shook his head.

"Hannah," he said. "You deserve someone who will give you their whole heart, and mine has already been given to Kate."

"What if she won't forgive you?" Hannah whispered.

"Then whoever I end up with, will have to accept that a piece of me is gone forever," Reed said.

Hannah looked out the windows, at the vast city that twinkled in the carpet of night. Reed watched her wrestle with what Reed had said and wondered if she'd react with anger, pushing him away and walling herself up again, the barricade even higher than before.

"You don't know how rare you are," Hannah finally said. "Before you even came to New York, I looked you up, and I knew you were different. I also knew you would have more in common with me than with Kate."

"It's not what you have in *common*," he said. "It's the *connection*. And you and I don't have it."

"But you left her behind," she said. "Why would you leave her behind if you cared that much about her?"

Stung, Reed shook his head. "It's not that simple. By the time I realized what she meant to me, it was too late. I had no other options."

He spoke the truth but it sounded flat in his ears, and he wondered again why he'd chosen to leave. The same wall he'd fought against for months appeared, but viewed after feeling Kate's absence for weeks it seemed weaker, vulnerable.

"Do you really love her?" Hannah asked.

"More than I can say," Reed said.

Hannah looked away and then back. "Then why are you standing here with me?"

"You did pretend to be her," Reed said, allowing a small smile.

She laughed and wiped the tears from her eyes. "I think this is the point where I say I'm sorry." More tears appeared and then she spoke in a whisper. "I really am."

"I know," he said. "And I'm sorry I can't be the guy you deserve."

She opened her arms to offer an embrace. "I think I'd like to be friends."

"Are you going to kiss me?" he asked, not entirely feigning fear.

"No more games," Hannah said.

Reed stepped in and hugged her, careful to keep enough distance to prevent it from feeling intimate. She clung to him, but made no motion to close the gap further. When they parted her smile was tentative.

"Is it going to be awkward working together now?"

"I'd prefer not," he said. "Because I really like what we're doing."

"Me too," she said.

They turned together and walked toward the elevator. Reed couldn't be certain, but he thought he saw her keep her own distance, as if she wanted to prove she wouldn't try anything else.

They rode the elevator down together, and halfway down he asked her about the next week's work. The question was an invitation for a conversation among friends, and she seemed to interpret it that way. But when they reached the line of taxis she smiled and turned to him.

"I'll take my own cab home," she said.

He grinned at her use of his own phrase. "I'll see you soon," he said.

They said goodbye and he got into his own cab, surreptitiously watching her climb into another. The action was not needed, but he recognized it as her first effort to show him that she would respect his boundaries.

"Where to?" the cabbie asked.

Reed went to answer *home*, but Hannah's questions bubbled to the surface. Why was he here? His mind knew the answer but his heart refused to accept it, and abruptly he jerked his head. Instead of the brownstone, he gave a different answer.

"The airport," he said. "I have a flight to catch."

Chapter 10

On the way to the airport Reed furiously looked up flights on his phone and found one that left that night. Then he checked his account and realized he didn't have enough for the ticket. Grimacing, he reconsidered his choice before jerking his head in the negative. Then he called Jackson.

"Hey," Jackson said.

"I need a favor," Reed said, and explained what he needed.

"It's about time," Jackson said.

Reed grinned and used Jackson's credit card to buy his plane ticket. He finished just as the cab came to a stop at the airport. As he got out he called Dr. Dickson next, and steeled himself for the conversation to come.

"Reed?" he asked. "Is everything all right?"

"I'm afraid not," Reed said, and told him about Hannah's picture, and how he'd resolved things with her. Then he braced himself. "This internship means more than I can express, and I know you've given me far more than I deserve. However, I need to ask you for two favors."

"What are the favors?" he asked.

"I need the next two days off," Reed said.

"That's a big request," Dr. Dickson said.

"I know," Reed said, stepping to the front of the line to print his ticket. "But there's something I need to do and I can't do it from New York."

"What's the second?" he asked.

His ticket in hand, Reed strode to the security line and outlined his second favor. When he finished there was silence on the line and Reed felt a burst of fear. He knew he was gambling everything on Dr. Dickson's confidence, a risk that could very well end his career.

He recognized that he stood on a precipice, the type of moment that an entire life hung in the balance. But Reed was committed. He wanted Kate. For now and for the future, even if it cost him his job.

"I'll have to ask about the second one," Dr. Dickson said. "It's not really up to me."

"I know," Reed said. "But I would really appreciate it."

"Two days," Dr. Dickson finally said. "But you have to make them up over the weekend. If you aren't at work on Saturday, I'll assume you chose a different priority."

"Thank you," Reed said, relief burning the fear from his veins. "I won't let you down."

"I know you won't," Dr. Dickson said. "Now go get her—but be back on Saturday."

"Thank you," Reed said.

"One more thing," he said, his voice turning serious. "Should you choose to remain in Boulder, I won't be able to help you again. Do you understand?"

"I understand," Reed said. "Thank you again."

"Good luck," he replied.

Reed hung up and suddenly realized his whole body was rigid. He released a long breath, struggling to contain the surge of hope. He thought his fate was sealed but now he'd been given two days.

Better make them count.

He texted Jackson the time he would be arriving and then enduring the questions as to why he had no bag. He wasn't surprised when security searched him. Then he hurried to his gate and boarded the plane.

It was odd taking a flight with no luggage or bags, and a few people noticed. He did have a few clothes and things he'd left in Boulder, items he hadn't thought he would need. It wasn't ideal but he hadn't wanted to stop at the brownstone, not when he felt such a rush. Besides, he'd always planned ahead for Kate. Not this time. As the plane backed away from the terminal he got a text from Hannah.

You okay? I thought you'd be back by now.

Reed texted back quickly. **You were right. I'm going to Boulder.**

Tonight??!!

Already on the plane, Reed said. Then he frowned and added. **Please don't post it to Ember's Blog**. He finished with an emoji to soften the comment.

Are you coming back?

I hope so, Reed replied.

For a moment there was no reply, and Reed grimaced, glancing at the flight attendants that were asking everyone to turn their phones to airplane mode. Just as he was about to turn his phone off, Hannah texted one more time.

Don't come back without her.

Reed grinned. **I won't.**

Reed turned off his phone just as the flight attendant walked by, and then settled in for the flight. Nervous and excited, he fidgeted until he remembered how much still needed to be done, and then settled in to plan.

73

The flight was long but he had a lot to do. He used his phone to scribble ideas, trashing those he deemed unsuitable. Tomorrow night was Valentine's Day, the anniversary of his first date with Kate, and he wasn't about to leave her hanging.

"What are you doing?" the girl next to him asked.

He glanced to her, realizing for the first time that he was sitting with two sisters. They were obviously in high school, their uniforms suggesting they were athletes. A handful of other girls in nearby seats were also in uniforms. The logo on the arm indicated they were the Eagles.

"Planning a date," he said.

"You've been planning a date for the last two hours?" she asked.

"Trying to," he said. "But this one is has a lot riding on it."

"What makes this date so important?" another girl asked.

"The girl," he said with a smile.

"So you're planning something big," she said, and pointed to the phone. "I mean, hot air balloons aren't normal for a date."

"True," Reed said. "But tomorrow night is special."

Her sister looked up and pulled off her headphones. "Because it's Valentine's Day?"

"That, and it's the anniversary of our first date," he said. "I met her last year."

"What did you do?" a girl across the aisle asked, pausing her movie.

He briefly described his first date with Kate, of the moment he'd arrived on her doorstep, of taking her to where he'd stashed dinner on the mountain, and then the downhill boating. By the time he was finished, two more Eagles were listening.

"And you did all that for a blind date?" a brunette asked.

"It's not that unusual," he said. "I've been dating her for a year now and we've sort of been doing a dating challenge to see who can plan the better date."

"That's *adorable*," the first sister said, her tone drawing the attention of her teammates, who chorused for more information.

Reed hesitated, but couldn't resist their expressions, so he obliged, telling his suddenly rapt audience of his second date with Kate. They clamored for more and he described each of his dates, from the St. Patrick's Date to the Marathon Date. As he did an idea began to form.

He mulled it over, testing it for problems and found that he liked it. By the time he finished his story of their dating challenge, the entire team was crowded around him, leaning over seats in order to listen.

"I can't believe you would do so much for her," one girl said, waving her hands over her eyes. "It's so sweet I think I'm going to cry."

"Wait," one of the girl's said. "Are you flying back just to take her on a date?"

Reed smiled. "You want me to tell you everything?" That sent them into titters, but before they could ask more he leaned closer. "I think there's actually something you can do for me, if you want to help."

"What do you want us to do?" one of them asked, eager.

"You live in Denver, right?"

One of the girl's nodded, "North side."

Reed lowered his voice and described what they could do. Their excitement quickly spread to action as they all pulled out their phones, and Reed was suddenly grateful for onboard wifi. As they went to work Reed returned his attention to his phone, finalizing his plans as the plane descended into Denver.

While they taxied to the terminal Reed listened to his impromptu army of high school teenagers work the phones like a seasoned sales team. When they deplaned he found himself engulfed in hugs and promises to participate.

When he was finally alone Reed looked at his phone and prepared himself for the hardest call yet. He'd put it off because more than anyone else, one girl had the power to make or break his plans. Taking a breath, he called Ember.

The phone rang twice and he half expected her to ignore the call. But that was not Ember's style. She would have glared down a charging bull rather than avoid a conflict, and on the third ring she picked up.

"I told you what I'd do if you broke her heart."

"You'd break my legs."

Her tone darkened. "I wasn't joking."

"I know," Reed said. "But I need your help."

"And what makes you think I would do anything for you?"

"Because you know I didn't cheat on Kate," Reed said. "Even without my explanation, you know Hannah orchestrated that picture because she wanted us to break up."

She sniffed. "I know nothing."

Ember wasn't shouting, and that was tantamount to an invitation, so Reed forged ahead. "I need you to get her to pick up when I call."

"Is that all?"

"And I need your help with one last invite."

"You think you can call from New York and demand I help you?" she asked, heat threading into her voice. "There's not a chance in—"

"I'm in Denver," Reed interrupted, hoping to forestall the inferno before it could reach through the phone and burn his face. "I just landed."

"I don't believe you," Ember said suspiciously.

Reed noticed a woman at a nearby terminal pick up the mic, so he put his phone on speakerphone and held it up. The woman at the desk called for flight 2814 to board, and when she was finished, Reed put the phone back to his ear.

"You could have faked that," she said.

"Ember," Reed said. "*Please*. You know I love her, and you know I would never hurt her."

"But you *did* hurt her," she said.

Reed could practically see her jut her chin out, her expression belligerent. "Kate's afraid," Reed said. "She's afraid that Hannah or a girl like her will take me away. So I'm here to prove just how much I love her."

There was silence on the line and Reed held his breath, not daring to hope. Asking Ember to help was like convincing the Incredible Hulk to star in a romantic comedy. She could just as easily destroy the set and smash everyone involved.

"What are you going to do?" she finally asked.

Reed pumped his hand into the air but managed to keep the shout inside, his sudden violence causing nearby flyers to look at him strangely. Swallowing the surge of confidence, he lowered his voice.

"I'm going to invite her to New York," he said.

"And just how is she going to do that?" Ember asked.

"Trust me," Reed said, a slow smile spreading on his face. "I have a plan."

Chapter 11

The days leading up to Valentine's Day passed in a sea of faces, and Kate hardly spoke. Numb to her bones, she struggled to accept what Reed had done. And what she had done in response. Like two warring factions, her anger and her love battled for dominance.

Reed messaged several times, and called when he knew she was not in class. At one point she sat and stared at the screen, willing herself to answer, but the image of Reed and Hannah remained fresh in her mind, and her hand did not move.

Her roommates tried to talk to her but she escaped into her room, locking the door for good measure. She overheard Ember talking about breaking the door down but Brittney and Marta convinced her otherwise, and the door remained intact.

She sat against the wall and held her knees, the creeping numbness preventing any tears. When Reed had left because of Aura she'd been broken, but now her loss was frequently pierced by bursts of anger. Reed was supposed to be the one she could always trust, and now she felt betrayed.

The previous snowstorm had partially melted, leaving the city blanketed in slush, the piles of dirty ice and water matching her soul. She trudged to her car and went to class, occasionally stopping to grind a piece of white snow into grey.

On Thursday her roommates invited Jackson and Shelby for a movie night, but at the last minute Jackson said he wasn't feeling well and stayed home. Shelby arrived after dinner and the group settled in to watch an old Indiana Jones movie, one of Shelby's favorites.

"Are you coming, Kate?" Shelby asked.

"No, thank you" Kate said, stepping to her room.

"You can't mope forever," Ember said. "And it's only a matter of time until you forgive him."

"I'm not going to forgive him," Kate said.

Ember laughed derisively. "He didn't cheat on you."

Kate's expression hardened. "You saw the picture."

"It looked like Hannah assaulted him," Shelby said. "And the way he smiled? You could tell he was uncomfortable."

"I agree," Brittney said, entering the room with the treat of the night.

"If I join you for the movie, will you stop talking about it?"

"Deal," Ember said, stabbing a finger at the empty seat.

Kate sighed and sank onto the chair, her anger at her friends fading back into the numbness that had dominated the last few days. Her roommates knew what had happened, but they did not know the truth. Kate had trusted Reed to hold his walls, and the fact that Hannah had gotten that close, showed that some walls could be breached. As much as she fought it, the picture that came to mind was of Hannah entering Reed's bedroom and removing her clothes . . .

A phone rang and Ember fumbled for it. The movie was one of Ember's favorites, and she had a smile on her face when she lifted her phone. Then she scowled like she was about to talk to her accountant.

"Who is it?" Kate asked.

Ember shook her head as she answered. "I told you what I'd do if you broke her heart."

Kate went rigid, ice dumping into her heart. Shelby and Brittney looked at her, and Shelby mouthed Reed's name. They'd run out of ice cream the day after the breakup and they'd resorted to cheese. Because

79

cheese. Kate had a piece of pepper jack in her hand and it lay forgotten as she listened to Ember's conversation.

It had taken all of her willpower to ignore Reed's calls and messages, but every time she wanted to give up, she remembered Reed's smiling face, Hannah draped on him like a buxom temptress.

"But you *did* hurt her," Ember said, her eyes flicking to Kate.

The fact that he'd called Ember could have been desperation but that was not what Kate got out of the call. Kate was privately pleased that Reed would risk Ember's ire in order to get to her. It showed he was willing to brave no small measure of fire.

Perhaps it was the Indiana Jones movie they were watching, but she felt oddly like the treasure at the end of the tomb, and Ember was the vengeful boulder just waiting to crush the intrepid explorer.

"Count me in," Ember finally said.

Kate's numbness turned to shock as Ember hung up and turned to Kate. For a moment there was silence, and Kate abruptly realized the movie was still playing. Shelby hastily fumbled for the remote and hit pause.

"What does he want?" Kate finally asked.

"You," Ember said with a smirk.

Kate grimaced. "You know what he did."

"Do you really think he cheated on you?" Shelby asked. "This is Reed we're talking about—the most honorable guy I've ever met—including Jackson, who is the one I'm going to marry."

"I can't get that picture out of my mind," Kate said.

"You've wallowed long enough," Brittney said, and when Kate looked at her she shrugged apologetically. "It's true. We all know you love him."

"He kissed another girl," Kate said, the statement tasting like bile. "It took him *six months* to kiss me." She stood up and picked up the cheese plate before walking into the kitchen.

"*She* kissed *him*," Brittney said, "and for all we know, Hannah staged it just to spite you."

"Girls can be like that," Shelby said. "Last week a girl told me she had sex with Jackson in my car."

"Did she?"

"Of course not," Shelby said, like the question was absurd. "She's liked Jackson for years and keeps trying to seduce him. I guess she thought making me jealous might work."

"You don't understand," Kate said, putting the plate down and leaning against the counter with a sigh. "I feel like I can't trust him anymore."

"You should," Ember said. "Because he's the best guy you're ever going to meet."

Kate turned to her and raised an eyebrow. "*You* think I should trust him?"

"Yes," Ember said.

"You did say he deserved to see his leg hair ripped off with hot wax," Shelby said.

Ember shrugged. "A girl has the prerogative to change her mind. Just like Kate should. Right now."

Kate looked between her friends. "Do you *all* think I should forgive him?"

"Yes," Brittney said.

"Definitely," Shelby said.

Ember pointed to Kate's pocket. "Pick up when he calls, Kate. Or you'll never forgive yourself."

For the first time in three days, Kate's heart thawed, and a small smile appeared on her face. Her friends, sensing the obvious, exulted as Kate pulled out her phone. Reed's name popped up as he called and she reached to answer. Then she thought better of answering in front of her roommates and strode to her bedroom door.

"Come on!" Ember called. "I let you listen."

"Thanks for that," Kate said as she shut the door.

She began to sit and then stood, pacing for a moment before calling Reed. The single ring seemed to go on forever and she almost hung up, but the moment it clicked she knew she was committed.

"Kate."

His voice all but melted her into the floor, and tears welled up in her eyes. She wanted to stay angry, to punish him for the slight, but all her anger evaporated, leaving her struggling to control the surge of relief.

"Reed," she said, grateful her voice did not tremble.

"I've been trying to call," Reed said.

"I know," she replied coolly, and then bit her finger to keep from revealing the burst of excitement. How could he make her melt with just his voice?

"Thank you for calling me back."

"Where's Hannah?"

"We had a talk," Reed said. "And I worked it out."

"How did you manage that?"

"I told her the truth," he said.

. . . please come to gate 47 . . .

The loudspeaker voice was in the background but unmistakable, causing Kate to frown. "Where are you?"

"Nowhere of consequence," he said.

Her eyes narrowed. "I thought you said you'd never lie to me."

"I won't," he said. "But sometimes I have to delay the truth in order to surprise you."

"I think that's still lying," she said.

"Let's call it a gray area," he replied matter-of-factly.

She reclined on her bed, the motion just like she had a hundred times while talking to him. It felt comfortable, not because of her posture, but because she was with Reed. He heart burned in her chest like a bonfire that had ignited, and her smile could not be constrained.

"It wasn't really fair to use Ember," Kate said.

"Are you kidding?" Reed asked. "Convincing her to turn to my side was harder than getting into college."

"She can be rather stubborn," Kate said. "But be warned, owing a favor to Ember can be costly."

"Then maybe I shouldn't have asked for two," he said.

"What's the second?" she asked suspiciously.

"I can't tell you that."

She heard the smile in his voice and, and the image burned the last of her regret from her chest. "I missed you," she said softly.

"And I love you," he replied.

"When do I find out what you're up to?"

"What day is tomorrow?" he countered.

"Valentine's Day," she said, and couldn't resist the smile. "And the anniversary of our first date."

"Did you really think I'd let you be alone on Valentine's Day?" he asked.

"You're in New York," she said, and then frowned as she recalled what she'd overheard. "Unless you're not . . .?"

"I don't know what you're talking about," Reed said. "But just make sure tomorrow night is free."

"I'll be waiting," Kate said.

They said their goodbyes and she hung up. For several moments she stared at the ceiling with a stupid grin on her face, wondering what Reed was up to. She could have sworn he was at an airport, but there's no way he could just leave the internship. Was there?

Abruptly she stood and strode into the living room. The movie was still paused and her friends were still talking, all going quiet the moment Kate appeared. She grinned, and without a word they knew.

"You're back with Reed!" Brittney cried, closing the gap to hug her.

"Was it ever a question?" Ember asked with a self-satisfying nod.

"You had me worried," Shelby said, coming around the couch and wrapping her arms around both of them.

Just then Marta swung the door open and took off her jacket. "Sorry I'm late," she said. "My aunt was sick and I had to close . . ." Her eyes swept the room and noticed Shelby and Brittney hugging Kate. "What happened?"

"Reed called Ember," Kate said.

"And Kate called Reed," Shelby said.

Marta's eyes flew to Kate and she burst into a teary smile. Crossing the room in a sprint, Marta engulfed Kate in an embrace, her words lost in the folds of her sweater. Ember grunted in irritation.

"You act like it's a surprise. We all knew she'd end up with Reed, and the blondes are always right."

Kate extracted herself. "You know about my nickname for you?"

"Of course," Ember said. "And now that we have Shelby, we're a force to be reckoned with."

"I'm one of the blondes?" Shelby asked in surprise.

"You are *actually* blonde," Brittney said. She reached out and flipped Marta's brown hair.

"I won't hold that against you," Ember said with a laugh.

Kate joined in, the amusement washing away the last three days of despair like waves over a sand castle, smoothing any lingering resentment and leaving her whole. These were her sisters, the girls that had been with her, supported her, lifted her. They would do anything for her—including betray her.

"Let's get down to business," Kate said when the laughter ended. "I want to know what he's up to. No holding back, not this time." She let her gaze sweep her friends. "This time you're on my team."

Ember glanced at the others, who nodded their agreement. Then she nodded as well. "Reed is in Denver," she said. "And he's on his way here . . ."

Chapter 12

Reed waited outside the airport for his ride, but he was not idle. He had no bags, no house, no car, and less than twenty-four hours until the final date would begin. On top of the invitation for the date, he had the date itself to plan, both of which required enormous preparation. Deciding he'd better start with his friends, he called Caleb.

"Reed," he said. "What's going on?"

"What are you doing tomorrow night?"

"Just helping Dr. Caldin grade some papers," he said. "Why? How's New York."

"You want to help me with something?" Reed asked.

"Does it have to do with Kate?"

Reed smiled. "Of course."

"Then count me in."

"I'll also need you to call Dr. Caldin," Reed said. "I could use his help as well."

"Just how big is this invite going to be?" Caleb asked.

"Epic," Reed said. "At least I hope it will be."

"Just tell me what you need." Caleb sounded intrigued.

"Projectors," Reed said. "Lots of them."

"I'll see what I can do."

"Keep me posted," Reed said.

He hung up and called another friend, and then another. By the time Jackson arrived, he'd gotten things in motion. Jackson's truck pulled up and Reed climbed in. The moment the door shut, Jackson pulled back into traffic.

"Everything set?" Reed asked.

"No 'hi' or 'good to see you'?" Jackson asked. "I think I at least deserve a 'thank you so much for being the most epic friend of all time.'"

"Sorry," Reed said with a grin. "Thank you so much for picking me up and you are the most epic friend I've ever had."

"Of all time," Jackson corrected.

"Of all time and space in any universe or dimension."

Jackson smirked. "Done. And yes, everything is set. But I think Shelby might be suspicious."

"Why?"

Jackson passed over his phone. As they pulled into the traffic heading away from the airport, he read the most recent messages from Shelby. At first they were normal until the last three, which gained a note of probing.

When do you think you'll be back?

Any chance you could pick up something on your way here?

You're not responding, everything okay?

"Ember must have told Kate I'm here," Reed said.

"You think so?" Jackson asked. "Won't that ruin what you have planned?"

"Not necessarily," Reed said. "I didn't really tell her much."

Reed frowned as he reviewed the conversation. He'd told Ember he planned on asking Kate to come back with him to New York, but he doubted Ember would reveal that. Throughout the dating challenge Ember had shown a willingness to switch sides, but she'd never outright destroyed any plan. Still, he had to be sure . . .

He noticed his phone was nearly dead, so he plugged it into Jackson's car charger. He hesitated, wondering if would be tipping his hand. But if Ember told Kate about his invite, his entire plan would be ruined. Realizing he had no choice, he carefully crafted a message and reviewed it before hitting send.

Whatever happens, don't tell anyone that I'm going to invite Kate to New York.

The reply came faster than he expected. **I'm sorry, you've reached a member of the opposing team. Your request has been noted and agreed upon, but any further requests will be denied. Have a nice day . . .**

Reed laughed dryly and read the text to Jackson, who grinned. "Looks like Kate has formed her own side. What do you think she will do?"

"She can't do anything without knowing my plan for the date," Reed said. "She won't want to risk doing anything else. We need an informant."

"You realize she's going to be doing the same thing," Jackson said.

"I know," he replied, considering his options. "But I think I need you to be my leak. You slip a few things to Shelby and they will run with them. The trick will be not letting Kate know what we're doing."

"Who do you want to recruit from her side?" Jakcson asked. "We can't trust Ember."

"True," Reed said. "And we can probably rule out Tanner. She will have turned him."

"Brittney," Jackson said. "But she'll need an incentive."

Reed was nodding. "And I know just the incentive."

He pulled out his phone and dialed Caleb back. He picked up on the second ring. "I've gotten a few projectors, but you haven't given me much time."

"Sorry," Reed said, "but I have another request. I think you'll like this one."

"Oh?"

"I want to use you as payment," Reed said, "to turn one of Kate's roommates to our side."

Caleb laughed. "What sort of payment?"

"A date," Reed said. "I've thought before about setting the two of you up, but this seems to be the right time."

"What's she like?" Caleb hedged.

Reed and Jackson exchanged a look, and Reed said, "She's one of the best girls I've ever had the privilege of knowing."

"As long as she's willing to cook with me."

Jackson and Reed smirked in unison. "You have no idea what you are in for."

"This payment stands ready," Caleb said.

"Thanks," Reed said.

"Why are you thanking me?" Caleb countered. "You're hooking me up with a girl, and getting me out of grading papers. I think I'm the one that should be thanking you."

Reed laughed and thanked him anyway. As Jackson stopped at the gas station, Reed fielded a flurry of sudden calls, reports from those he'd called from the airport. Then Jackson got in and they headed north.

"Have you assembled the minions?" Jackson asked.

"Not all of them," Reed said. "But they seem to be getting together."

"What did Brittney say?" he asked, pulling onto the freeway.

"I was just about to message her," Reed said.

He considered the message and then typed it out, keeping it brief in case Brittney decided to share it with Kate. Brittney was the quietest of Kate's roommates, but in many ways the most loyal. Reed hoped to use her loyalty against her. He reread the message before he hit send.

I know what Kate is up to but she can't plan anything unless she knows the when and where of the date I'm planning. Will you help me?

The answer did not come immediately, and Reed imagined Brittney surreptitiously leaving the room to answer. When the reply came it was just what he expected.

Kate wants us to tell her everything.

I know, Reed responded. **But if she doesn't know anything, she can't plan either. Besides, I have a guy I'll set you up with if you help. He does creative dating . . .**

Are you trying to get me to betray my friend for a hot date?

To HELP your friend for a hot date. I promise I won't force you to spy too much.

When do I get paid?

On Valentine's Day, Reed promised.

Then you have your mole.

Reed grinned and read the conversation to Jackson, who pointed to his James Bond shirt. "I've always wanted to be in a spy movie."

Jackson pulled onto the freeway and merged into the traffic. It was already ten, so Reed debated how much more he could do tonight. He had a list of friends already working on gathering the supplies he would need and he could call anyone he'd forgotten tomorrow.

He was suddenly gripped by a surge of nervousness. The date he had in mind was the biggest he'd ever planned, but it was the ending that made him uneasy. A date wasn't good enough. Not this time. He wasn't going back to New York alone. But how would Kate respond to such a request? He was betting everything on Kate's willingness to come back to New York. If she refused, it would be a brutal statement as to the status of their relationship.

Could they survive such an answer? Could *he* endure such a rejection? Even in the dating challenge, he'd never invested himself so completely, shown such a vulnerability. He'd flown back to Boulder, called in every favor, enlisted the help of countless friends and would enlist even more, and if she said no . . .

He looked out the window, the lights of Denver gradually dimming as they left the city behind. They changed lanes to pass a semi, its large frame briefly blocking the view. By the time they had passed, the city had ended and there was only darkness.

Would his relationship end like that? Because he'd failed to see the signs of them falling apart? If she said no to his invitation it could shatter their relationship and he would go back to New York. Alone.

He jerked his head, unwilling to consider that possibility. He loved Kate—and he knew what she felt about him. But he would be asking Kate to drop out of school and move across the country, to put her career on hold as she applied to other schools. He was asking her to do the very thing he could not.

"What's wrong?" Jackson asked.

"What if she says no to New York?"

Jackson shook his head. "Why would she? She loves you and since you've gone to New York she's hated being apart."

"But I'm asking her to just drop out of school and leave."

"It's not too late to drop out without penalty," Jackson said. "She won't have to pay tuition."

"I know," Reed said. "But she will have to put her life on hold."

"Some things are more important than a career."

"Like Shelby?" Reed asked, glancing at him.

Jackson nodded. "A career serves a family. A family doesn't serve a career."

Reed raised an eyebrow. "That's very clever."

Jackson nodded sagely and then withdrew a slip of paper from a pocket in his door. "And you lucky numbers are 17, 23, and 4."

Reed laughed, the amusement rolling off him as he accepted the fortune and read the proverb Jackson had quoted. Jackson merely grinned smugly as he switched lanes to pass a minivan.

"Where did you get this?" Reed asked.

"I've been saving it," Jackson admitted. "I knew it would come in handy."

"How many fortunes do you have?" Reed asked.

"I don't have your memory," Jackson said defensively. "I needed something to give me an advantage."

Reed's smile faded. "But *I* wasn't willing to give up my career," he said.

"I know," Jackson said. "But for her to transfer to NYU will cost her what, one semester? For you to stay would have cost a whole lot more."

"You're brilliant, you know that?" Reed asked.

"That's what my mom said," Jackson said.

Reed laughed. "So you really think she'll say yes?"

"Of course," he said. "And don't worry, I'm on your side."

"What if Shelby tries to get it out of you?"

"I can resist for one night," Jackson said, and then pretended to cough. "Besides, I think I'm coming down with something."

"That will work," Reed said.

A text came in and Reed responded, grateful for the initial reports. He already had six projectors lined up but he needed more. He answered another call and then another text, and then he and Jackson began discussing the date itself. The drive to Boulder was the shortest Reed had ever experienced, and before he knew it they were getting off the exit. He'd expected it to feel like home, but there was only one home in Boulder that mattered, and it wasn't a house. Then he got a text from Brittney with an update, which he shared with Jackson.

"You realize you and Kate are both planning a date for tomorrow night," Jackson said as they pulled into the familiar driveway. "And this could blow up in your faces."

"It is a dating challenge," Reed said.

"So you think you can pull this off?"

Reed's smile spread across his face. "Two dates," he said. "One night."

Jackson's laugh was filled with anticipation. "Let the games begin . . ."

Chapter 13

Reed didn't sleep well, his excitement burning in his veins. It reminded him of the night before he'd gone to Disney World for the first time, when he'd thought of all the incredible things he was about to see. At the time he'd struggled to decide which park they would visit first. This time his entire life hung in the balance of a single night.

He gave up at six and left the couch. The apartment had changed significantly in the weeks of his absence, and Tanner had added movie posters to the wall. They were for old movies, and included two from Star Wars.

Reed borrowed Jackson's laptop and sat down at the kitchen table. Rubbing his face, he poured himself into action. He made a list first, and then noted who was doing which piece. This was his biggest date yet and it needed to be perfect.

He frowned when he looked at the list of names and realized he needed more help to pull it off. Picking up his phone, he began dialing. By the time Jackson plodded into the kitchen, Reed had reached out to dozens of friends, calling in every favor from his time at the university.

"You're up early," Jackson said with a yawn.

"Happy Valentine's Day," Reed said.

He grinned and flopped down onto the chair. "Thanks sweetheart."

He pulled out his phone and called Shelby, wishing her the same before hanging up and turning his attention to breakfast. Gathering his favorite cereals, he placed them on the table and then retrieved bowls from the cupboard.

"What are you doing for Shelby?" Reed asked.

"I snuck a bunch of flowers into her car," Jackson said.

"Roses?" Reed asked.

"That too," Jackson said, pouring himself a bowl. "I also put in a bunch of sports stuff as well."

"Why?"

"I wrote a note that said, 'Doesn't matter the sport, you're always my MVP.'"

"You guys are adorable," Reed said.

He stood and began to pace, ignoring the bowl Jackson had gotten for him. There were so many moving parts he couldn't keep it straight. He felt the need to focus, but the last time he'd focused exclusively on his relationship with Kate, he'd ignored Jackson. He would never again make Jackson feel like he didn't matter.

"What are you doing tonight?" Reed asked.

Jackson snorted, a slight smile on his face. "You've reached your support quota. Do you want to talk about what you have planned or not?"

"I don't mind," Reed said. "This is your first Valentine's Day with a fiancé."

Jackson's expression turned incredulous. "You're pacing so much you're making me nervous. Sit down and tell me what you've got."

Reed relented and sat. Between cramming cereal into his mouth he told Jackson what he'd managed to do since six, and laid out everything that still needed to be done. Jackson sat back and listened as he ate, his expression that of a seasoned spy.

"What intel has our informant given us?" Jackson asked.

"Brittney texted an hour ago to say that Kate believes Shelby's information. She won't tell me what she's doing, but at least we know— that Kate knows—the basic plan."

"But she doesn't know the ending, right?" Jackson asked.

"Not unless you told her," Reed said, his eyes narrowing.

Jackson feigned offence. "If you can't trust me, who can you trust?"

"I trust you to do what's best for me," Reed said, leaning forward in his chair. "Even if it's not what I ask."

Jackson fidgeted. "I told her exactly what you said I should."

"And *nothing* else?"

Reed stared Jackson down until he grimaced. "It's not my fault. Shelby threatened me with a month without—"

"What did you tell her?" Reed asked.

He smirked. "That you would be showing up at 6:00," Jackson said. "And that dinner was going to be at the observatory."

"Nothing about the stadium?" Reed pressed.

"Nothing," Jackson said. "I swear."

All things considered, it wasn't all bad. The observatory was the place of their first date, so it was almost expected. But he now had to assume that the location was compromised, and Kate would make her own plans around that location.

"I'm sorry," Jackson said, his tone apologetic. "On an unrelated topic, I've discovered Shelby owns me."

Reed laughed. "I can't blame you. She is going to be your wife. Just remember I want you to be a leak—not a gusher."

"Deal," he said.

Reed fleetingly considered if he should cut Jackson out, but knew he would never do it. Jackson was his best friend, a brother in everything but blood, and Reed needed someone he could trust—even if he might let slip a few extra secrets.

"I need to get to the observatory to meet a friend," Reed said. "Then I've got to connect with Caleb, who's on the projector committee."

"You have committees now?" Jackson asked.

"Five," Reed said with a smile.

"What about me?"

"You're on the 'don't betray me again' committee."

"Can I be the chairperson?"

"Done."

He grinned and saluted. "Yes, captain."

Reed stood and picked up his phone, which was already buzzing. "Ramon is dropping off my old car now, so I'll see you at lunch. I'll need your help to get into Kate's room this afternoon."

"I'll be here after my morning classes," he said, and then scowled. "Why doesn't every professor cancel class on Valentine's Day? Don't they understand how important it is?"

Reed grinned and strode to the door. "I'll see you at lunch."

He picked up the coat he'd found in the box he'd left behind and left. As he walked to the driveway he ran through the list he'd made, and for the first time, wondered if he was going too far. Then he thought of Kate and shook his head. No matter what, he needed her to understand how much he loved her.

He looked up when an engine snarled, and a car pulled into the driveway. The ancient Camry looked nothing like his old car. Ramon, Marta's cousin, had replaced the wheels with steel rims and the seats with red and black leather. The exterior was all black with sleek red stripes across the top. A spoiler above the trunk added to the look.

Reed shook his head in disbelief when Ramon drove the car onto the driveway and put it in park. His smug grin said it all as he exited and handed the keys to Reed, who stared at the incredible machine where it idled like a dragon on wheels.

"What did you do to my car?"

"*Your* car?" Ramon asked. "I added a few upgrades when it became *my* car."

"But it's only been a few weeks."

"I had been gathering the upgrades for a while," he said. "I just needed a Camry with a manual transmission."

"It's beautiful," Reed said.

"Not done yet," Roman said. "I've still got a pile of parts to finish putting on. Don't scratch it."

"I won't," Reed said, accepting the keys.

Reed got in and settled into the comfortable seats. Warm air blew from the vents, while a flashy stereo faded between colors. He rolled down the window and called out to Roman as he walked towards a car parking on the street.

"Does it fly?"

"Not yet!" he called with a laugh.

Reed grinned and shifted to reverse before backing out. The clatter from the fan and loose steering were gone, and the engine had been replaced by a beast. He cringed when he tapped the gas and the Camry surged forward as if eager to devour the road.

He carefully drove to the observatory and parked in the nearly full parking lot. Then he walked up the steps and inside, where a crowd of students were gathered. They noticed his arrival and began to clap, whereupon Lisa turned and smiled.

"Reed," Lisa said. "I see you've gathered a crowd."

"Thank you all for coming," he said, waving to all of them. "I know it's Valentine's Day so this means a lot to me. As you know, this is the final date, and I have a lot planned."

He noticed a number of those present were couples, plus many girls he'd taken on dates. They looked to their dates and back to him, the

98

eagerness evident on their faces. A knot of emotion climbed into Reed's throat as he saw them here to help.

"Think we can make this happen?"

"You think we'd bail now?" one asked, laughing like it was an absurd question.

"Lisa?" Reed said. "I can't thank you enough for doing this for me."

"Being the manager has its perks," Lisa said.

Lisa turned and surveyed the group like a foreman on a construction site. Of the twenty or so present, all were students, most from Reed's psychology department. Lisa had conscripted a handful of friends, and the excited group followed her into the observatory.

"The tools are on the table," Lisa said. "You'll find bolts holding the chairs down, but each has to removed individually. Please keep the bolts or my boss will have my head."

Reed rolled up his sleeves and dived in, helping to move the chairs to a storeroom nearby. His friends bombarded him with questions and he answered those he could, conscious of the fact that any one of them could be working for Kate.

Designed to be removed for special events, the auditorium chairs were gradually cleared. Occasionally someone had to leave to go to class or work, but more arrived, the room filling with people working, talking, and laughing. They took a break for lunch and Reed prepared to leave.

"Again, thank you," he said as they ate the pizzas he'd ordered. "And if you aren't busy, be at the stadium at 8:00 sharp. Otherwise, reach out to Caleb about the projectors he's collecting."

They came forward to wish him luck, pausing to say a few words of encouragement or give a hug. Most were familiar faces but some of those present he'd never met. It didn't matter, they were all eager to be part of the dating challenge.

Lisa walked him out. "We'll have it done in the next hour or so."

"Thank you," Reed said. "Oh, and Kate may try to call."

"Oh?" she asked. "Why would she do that?"

The smile on her face brought Reed to a halt. "She already called you."

"Maybe," Lisa said, and turned to her car. "Have a great night, Reed!"

Reed laughed, and wondered if he could get her to talk. Or if he wanted her to reveal what Kate had planned. Over the last year he'd come to love Kate's dates as much as his own, her flair for the creative making each surprise more clever than the last. As much as his curiosity mounted, he would not spoil it for her.

He checked the time and then hurried to Roman's car. As he drove home he called Caleb for an update, and then at his suggestion, Dr. Caldin, who had received permission to use the stadium. Reed breathed a sigh of relief, grateful that hurdle had been crossed.

"Thank you for the help," Reed said. "For everything. I'm sure you can watch the video on Ember's blog."

Dr. Caldin released the dry laugh Reed had heard so many times during class. "Mr. Thompson, if you think I would miss this, you are sorely mistaken. My wife and I will be there at eight."

Reed smiled. "I'll see you then."

He drove to Kate's house and parked around the block. Then he walked to her door, arriving just as Jackson appeared. Before they knocked, Brittney opened the door and ushered them inside.

"Hurry," she said. "I bought you an hour but they might come back early."

"Thanks Brittney," Reed said.

"I look forward to my payment!" she called, sprinting to her car and driving away.

Reed and Jackson carried four boxes from Reed's truck. They went to work in a flurry, rushing to finish Kate's room before she returned. Reed worked with a smile, the anticipation at seeing Kate's face driving him to heightened speed.

They finished and Reed checked the clock, wincing as he realized they were out of time. They loaded the empty boxes back into the truck and sprinted in for the last load. Just as they picked up the last two boxes a car pulled into the driveway. Reed shut the bedroom door to a crack just as the front door opened and Kate walked in.

She hung her keys on the rack and pulled out her phone. Then she began walking toward her bedroom. Reed frantically sought for a place to hide while Jackson stabbed a finger toward the window. But it was too late, and Kate's hand closed on the doorknob.

The doorbell rang and Kate turned. Reed breathed a sigh of relief and Jackson began opening the window. At the crack of the door, Reed watched Kate swing the door open to reveal her brother.

"Bake?" Kate asked. "What are you doing here . . .?"

Chapter 14

Her thoughts on Reed and the upcoming date, Kate swung the door open. To her surprise it was her brother, Baker, his towering frame blocking the afternoon sun. Delighted, she stepped into a bruising embrace.

"Bake?" Kate asked. "What are you doing here?"

"I was in Denver for training," he said, his eyes scanning the living room. "I figured I could stop by and surprise you."

Kate had grown accustomed to the perpetual wariness in her brother's eyes, a side effect of his time in Special Forces. But that caution did not extend to her, and he enveloped her in a crushing embrace.

"How long can you stay?" she asked.

"A few hours," he said. His eyes flicked to her bedroom door and narrowed, before returning to her. "You okay?"

"I'm fine," she said. "Why do you ask?"

"I heard about the picture on Ember's blog."

She frowned. "You're not going to kill him, are you?"

"Probably not," Baker said. He didn't smile.

"Please don't," she said. "Things have changed in the last day." She motioned him inside but he jerked his head.

"Why don't we take a walk?"

Taken aback by the request, she gestured to the door. "It's warming up but it's still just fifty degrees."

"The heat of Afghanistan never really leaves the bones," Baker said wryly. "And I find the cold refreshing."

Anxious to ease his concerns and keep Reed intact, Kate agreed and grabbed her coat. Then she stepped outside and they strolled to the sidewalk. The slush had all but melted, leaving patches of lingering snow on some lawns. The season was not as warm as last year, when Valentine's Day had hit the high forties, but it was still warmer than usual.

"Kate," Baker said. "What's going on?"

"Reed came back," she said.

"You've seen him?"

"Not yet," she said. "He flew in last night, or that's what I've been told."

"I thought he had to stay in New York for a year."

"He does," she said. "But something happened that changed things."

She wondered if she should talk about Hannah, but thought better of it. Bake might think she blamed Reed. The last time they'd met, her brothers had kidnapped Reed in the middle of the night and gotten him into a knife fight.

"How bad is it, Kate?"

She grimaced at the darkness to his tone, hoping to he wouldn't harm Reed. "It wasn't as serious as I first thought."

"You decided to take a break," he said casually.

She came to a halt and turned to face him. "How are you so well informed? Do you follow Ember's blog?"

"I don't blog," he said flatly. "But mom does, and she told a great deal."

103

"So you did see the picture?"

"I wish I hadn't," he said, his voice dropping several degrees.

"Please don't do anything to Reed."

Baker looked away, and then back. "I don't think I will," he said. "He showed me his caliber, and when that girl kissed him on the cheek, I suspect he used his words to put her in her place. That's more his style."

Baker admired grit and physical strength as much as intelligence, so describing someone in such a fashion would normally have been an insult. But his tone was respectful. Reed may not have used the same weapons as Baker, but he still saw him as a warrior.

"So you like him?"

"How can I not?" Baker said. "He's the first truly decent guy you've dated. He needs some combat training, but I can cover that part. Honor and integrity are hard to teach." He frowned. "But don't tell him I said that. Fear can be useful."

"I don't think he's afraid of you," Kate said.

Baker surprised her with a chuckle. "Maybe not, but only because I'd have to go through you to reach him."

She couldn't argue with that. "What you think of him is really important to me."

"It's nice, seeing you so excited about a guy," he said.

"I'm in love with him," Kate said, a smile rising to her lips. "And I want to stay with him."

"What does that mean?" Baker asked.

She hesitated, and then realized it didn't matter if Baker knew. He would never tell Reed. "I'm going to ask him to come back to Boulder."

"You think he'd give up his future for you?"

She grimaced. "I'm hoping he sees me as his future. Do you think he'll want to be with me?"

Baker held her gaze, surprise on his features. "That's not a question a girl usually asks her older brother."

"I know," Kate said. "But you know my relationship with Reed has been different from the start, and this is the only way I can show him how much I love him."

"And if he says no?" Baker asked.

Kate sensed the weight to the question, and the cold wind seemed to pierce her coat and chill her heart. What she wanted to ask him would be huge, and drastically affect his career and life. Just asking would be opening her heart and leaving her at her most vulnerable. If he said no . . .

She shuddered, and realized that if he did refuse, it could shatter their relationship. He would return to New York and she would be alone. And broken. Was a future with Reed worth the potential cost? Worth the risk?

Yes.

The answer was quick in coming, thawing the icy fear that had briefly gripped her. Her future hung on the request, but this was Reed, and she would sacrifice anything to be with him. She just hoped he was ready to do the same.

"He won't say no," she said.

Baker regarded her for a long moment, measuring her resolve. "You may not be a soldier, little sis, but I wish you were. If you want to do this, I have your back."

"Thank you," Kate said, tears coming to her eyes as she embraced him.

"However," he said. "I think I'll stick around until tonight. I want to see how this turns out."

"So you can kill him if he says no?"

He shook his head. "If he says no, he's not the man I thought he was."

Kate nodded in agreement, but her hope would not yield to fear again, and so she turned back towards her house. Baker walked her home but slowed as they approached the house and pulled out his phone.

"I need to let my CO know I'll be getting in late tonight," he said. "I'll catch up with you later today?"

"I'll try," Kate said, "But I'm going to be busy. There's a lot going on."

"I understand," he said. "But something tells me I'll see you before the night is over."

He gave a mysterious smile before walking to his car. Confused, Kate wondered just how much her brother knew, and then realized it didn't matter. She had her own plans to finish, so she turned and walked into her house. As she did she called Ember, who was probably just getting out of class.

"What's our status?" she asked.

"Everything's coming together," Ember said. "With Shelby's information I've reached out to the right people. But I'm hearing whispers that Reed is going to end the night at the stadium."

"Dig up what you can," she said.

She entered the living room and for the second time in half an hour, hung up her coat. Then she strode to her bedroom and swung the door open. She froze, her words trailing off as she stared.

A projector had been placed vertically on the floor, the image bouncing off hanging mirrors to flood the room with light. Stars, planets, even a comet, soared across her walls and ceiling, lifting her small bedroom into the infinite cosmos.

"Kate?" Ember asked. "What's going on?"

"Reed left an invite," she breathed.

"Where?"

"In my bedroom," Kate said.

"It wasn't me," Ember said. "It must have been Marta or Brittney who helped him . . ."

"I don't care," Kate said, staring in awe at the scene.

"I'm on my way," Ember said, and hung up.

Kate hardly noticed, and she slowly entered the room and shut the door. With thick curtains covering the window, the only light came from the projector, and she turned a slow circle, basking in Reed's invitation.

Two of of the comets collided, and where they shattered words began to appear, the letters forming into a single sentence that covered the bare wall. Overcome with emotion, she read it aloud.

"An eternity with you would not be enough. Will you be my date for Valentine's Day?"

It finished with his name and a time, and the location she already knew. The observatory. The words faded away and the celestial view returned. She pulled out her phone and dialed Reed, and wasn't surprised when he picked up on the first ring.

"I hope this isn't a distance date," she said, and realized she was speaking softly, unwilling to disturb the serenity of her room.

"And what makes you think it won't be?" he teased.

"This room," she said, sweeping her hand at the stars and planets soaring past her. "Jackson may have helped set this up, but it has your style."

"I have a style?" he asked.

"You do," she said with soft laugh. "So please tell me I get to see you today."

"I think we both know the answer to that," he said. "And I suspect you already knew where the date was going to start."

She giggled, abruptly overcome with a desire to see him. "I'm not even sure what I can trust anymore."

"Let our friends have their fun," Reed said. "They've been part of our challenge too, so they deserve to see the end."

"So today's the end of the challenge?" she asked.

"A final date," he said. "After that, who knows?"

She swallowed at the simmering smile in his voice. "I'll see you at six," she said. "But don't start thinking you've won this yet. It's not over."

"I already won," he said. "I have you."

Her smile widened and her heart fluttered against her ribs. She wondered how it was possible to feel so much at once, to love someone so much. It felt like she could reach out and touch his hand, feel the gentle caress of his fingers. She trembled and then managed to speak.

"I'll see you at six."

"I'll be the handsome one in a suit," he said.

A laugh escaped her lips. "You don't need a suit to be handsome."

He laughed in turn and they said their goodbyes. She remained in place, marveling at the invitation he'd left in her bedroom. Many of his invitations had required more work to set up, but today felt different, the implication that the night harbored more than fun.

Ember burst into the room and came to a halt, for once stunned to silence. A few minutes later Brittney and Marta joined them and the foursome watched the stars unfold and the invite appear.

"I hate to say it," Marta said. "But I think his is better."

"Than ours?" Ember shook her head. "He knows more of what is happening tonight. Kate's invite is flawless."

"When will he see it?"

"He should find it any minute," Kate said, glancing to Marta.

"Shelby and I finished after you left," Marta said, her eyes gleaming. "It shouldn't be long now . . ."

Chapter 15

Reed and Jackson huddled in Kate's bedroom, and he watched Kate speak to Baker. Then Baker's eyes flicked to her bedroom door. Reed's heart sank as he realized Baker knew they were there.

"He knows we're here," Reed whispered.

"How?"

"He has the hearing of superman," Reed replied.

"And the body," Jackson said. "He's built like a cement truck."

"*Why don't we take a walk . . .*" Baker said.

Reed's eyes widened. "He's going to let us escape."

A moment later Baker confirmed his comment. Kate reached for her jacket and Baker turned to the bedroom door. He raised his hands to show all five fingers, and then stabbed a finger towards the back of the house.

"We have five minutes," Reed said. "Out the window."

The front door shut and they retreated out the back window. Before they left, Reed turned on the projector and took a moment to see the invite. Molly, a girl he'd taken on a date once, had made the video. She was gifted in graphic design and she'd been one of his calls the previous night.

"You've outdone yourself, Molly," he murmured and then turned to Jackson, who was halfway out the window.

Reed handed him the empty boxes and then climbed out himself. The backyard was fenced and small, the grass piercing the patches of lingering snow. They hurried to the gate and eased it open before Reed poked his head out. He looked down the street and spotted Baker and Kate just starting their walk back, so Reed motioned Jackson toward the back fence.

They reached the back fence and both climbed over. Then they hurried through the neighbor's yard and circled the block to Jackson's truck. They reached the truck just as Reed's phone rang, and he motioned Jackson to silence.

"I hope this isn't a distance date," she said when he answered.

Reed grinned and leaned against the truck. The usual banter was lighter than normal as they both pretended not to know that Reed was in town. He imagined her standing in the room where they'd nearly been caught, and the previous tension was replaced with anticipation.

Jackson finished loading their things into the truck bed and then motioned to the cab, a questioning look on his face. Reed shook his head, not wanting her to realize how close they really were to the house.

"I'll see you at six," she said.

"I'll be the handsome one in a suit," he replied.

"You don't need a suit to be handsome," she said, her laugh making him imagine a blush climbing her cheeks.

He hung up and turned to Jackson, who was leaning against his truck. "I'm the smug one, remember?"

Reed grinned. "I think she liked it. But we're running out of time and there's a lot left to set up."

"Don't worry," he said. "I posted to Ember's blog."

"You what?" Reed asked, stopping as he reached for the door.

"You wanted as many people as you could get," he said with a shrug. "And she's got tons of followers."

"But what if Kate—"

"She hasn't looked at it since the Hannah picture," Jackson said with a dismissive wave. "You don't need to worry."

"Her roommates are going to see it," Reed said.

"I texted them too," he said. "But made clear it wasn't something Kate could know."

Reed frowned, but Jackson's plan made sense. Reed still needed help and there were only a few hours until the start of the date. It was also Valentine's Day, so asking people to show up to help him seemed a bit much.

"What does the post say?" he asked cautiously.

"A time and a place," he said. "That's all."

Before Jackson could continue Reed pulled out his phone and read the new message, snorting in amusement. Taking his silence as consent, Jackson grinned and folded his arms. When Reed finished the post he sighed and slipped his phone back into his pocket.

"Fine," he said. "It was a good idea. You ready to go now?"

"Not yet," a voice said.

They turned to find Baker standing next to them. Reed hadn't even heard him approach, yet Kate's oldest brother was suddenly standing just feet from them. How did a guy so large just appear without being noticed?

"Where did you come from?" Jackson asked, and then leaned over to Reed and lowered his voice. "Look out, he's got Batman skills."

"I could have killed you without you noticing I was here," Baker said, his tone amused. "Sneaking up on you is even easier."

"It's good to see you, too," Reed said with a smile.

"Do the skills come with the muscles?" Jackson asked. "Or or are they only part of the luxury package?" He reached out and poked Baker in the shoulder.

Reed half expected Baker to knock him to the ground, but instead he shrugged. "They're certainly not luxury upgrades."

"I knew it," Jackson said, looking down at his chest. "I shouldn't have gotten the standard model. I mean look at him, I bet you could crack a walnut between your pecks."

"Or a head," Baker said.

Jackson burst into a laugh and wrapped an arm around Baker. "Threats must be your love language. Mine's talking, and cold cereal. I really like cold cereal."

The muscular Jackson looked scrawny compared to Baker's steel body, and Reed held his breath, wondering if he was about to witness a fractured skull. Baker regarded Jackson with a look that would have sent any other men scurrying away, but Jackson didn't remove his arm.

"I like cereal too," Baker said, and Reed could have sworn he saw the ghost of a smile. "But I'm not here to make friends. Reed, do you have a minute?"

Reed checked the time nodded. "Now's a good time."

"Good."

Stepping free of Jackson, Baker walked away, and Reed caught up in three strides. They walked in silence until they were out of earshot of Jackson and then Baker turned and looked him up and down. Reed endured the scrutiny, waiting for Baker to speak first.

"I'm surprised you called after what went down with Hannah's picture."

"I'm surprised you drove up to Boulder."

Reed hadn't realized Baker was in Denver when he'd called the previous night. But he'd never expected Kate's oldest brother to drive up in person. Still, Reed hoped he had not come to shatter his spine.

"The answer is yes," Baker said.

Reed breathed a sigh of relief. "Thank you."

"Don't mention it."

"So we're good?"

"As long as you don't kiss another girl, I think we're good."

Reed grinned. "It won't happen again."

"It better not," Baker said. "But you should know Kate has her own plans for tonight. It might not go the way you think."

Confused, Reed glanced at Jackson but he obviously hadn't heard. As if he enjoyed the consternation he'd caused, Baker clapped him on the shoulder—nearly knocking him from his feet—and then turned away.

"I'll be at the stadium tonight," he said. "Good luck."

He turned and strode away, leaving Reed to his confusion. Then he walked back to Jackson and filled him in on the strange conversation. As they climbed into the truck and drove away, Jackson shook his head.

"I like him."

"He doesn't scare you?"

"Like I'm a six year old facing a ravenous tiger in the woods," Jackson said calmly.

Reed snorted in amusement. "I can't believe you touched him and kept your arms."

"It wasn't the best move on my part," Jackson mused. "But I tend to panic when I meet someone that could rip my heart out with his pinky finger."

Reed picked up his phone and then texted several more people, the time becoming a major factor in his plans. Calls and messages were flooding in from people wanting to help, and Reed was hard pressed to answer them all.

Despite his rush, Reed continued to ponder the brief conversation with Baker. Kate had obviously spoken to Baker, and shared things he didn't know. What was she setting up? And how could it interfere with tonight's plans?

For the first time a spark of worry darkened his hope. He'd returned to Boulder with a plan, one Kate had hijacked for her own purposes. Initially Reed had thought the idea of them both battling for dominance on the final date would be fun, but now he considered the idea they might have conflicting goals.

He was pulled from his thoughts when they rounded the corner and his old house came into view. Shock bound his tongue and he leaned forward in his seat. The truck slowed down and Jackson too leaned forward.

"What in the . . ."

A small crowd was gathered around the house, pointing and taking pictures of the windows, where balloons were visible, packed together so tightly they reached the ceiling. And it wasn't just the living room.

Jackson was forced to park a block away and they got out. Reed was recognized immediately, with neighbors and friends calling out his name as he walked through the crowd. Many took video on their phones and he smiled and nodded to them on the way to the door.

"I thought we had the upper hand," Jackson said.

"I thought we did too," Reed said, and reached for the handle. "But it looks like Kate planned her own invitation."

"This is Tanner's handiwork," he said. "And I thought he was on our side."

"He's dating Ember," Reed said. "I don't think he had a choice."

Jackson grinned and retreated a step. "Go ahead."

Reed looked back to the crowd and raised his voice. "You ready?"

"Yes!" they chorused.

Reed pulled the door open—and balloons exploded out. They engulfed him and cascaded down the steps, bouncing away to fill the street. Some were helium and they floated into the sky, while others were caught in the wind and tumbled away.

Balloons *filled* the house. From floor to ceiling, wall to wall, they were so dense Reed couldn't even see the door to his old room, and the kitchen was lost in a sea of color. Then he noticed the note on the door.

One of me is not like the other

Find me and I'll be yours forever

Reed waded in, trying not to trip as the balloons shifted like a sentient mass, swallowing him whole. He fumbled his way through, struggling to find the one balloon that didn't look like the others. Laughter came from outside as children charged the tidal wave of balloons exiting the front door, their cries of delight muted by the mass of balloons.

"Are you lost?" Jackson called.

"Yes!" Reed shouted.

Then he saw it. Nestled just inside the door to his old room, one balloon was different than the rest, and he pushed his way to it. Wading through an ocean of balloons was shockingly fun, and a smile spread on his face as he hunted. Then he grasped the base of a massive balloon. It was so large he had difficulty fitting it through the door, and he tugged and pulled it back to the front door. He emerged with the giant balloon and the crowd cheered.

"Looks like there's a note inside," Jackson said.

Reed spotted the scrap of white and called out. "Plug your ears!" then he withdrew his car keys and used them to pop the balloon.

Everyone winced as the giant balloon burst, allowing a large piece of paper to flutter to the ground. Reed picked it up and carefully unfolded it. He read it once and then read it aloud, his voice carrying over the children still playing in the yard.

A thousand balloons for a thousand dates

All of which I hope to be mine

The challenge may end but our life begins

If you'll be my Valentine

Reed turned the note so the crowd could read it. "What do you think? Should I accept?"

The shouts were all the answer he needed, and he smiled, abruptly overcome with how many supported the dating challenge. From the beginning, others had shown a willingness to assist in dates and activities, always willing to be part of their romance. Some of those present had likely helped blow up the balloons. And how many would be at the stadium tonight?

At first he'd wondered why, but as he surveyed the group he realized that love was not an emotion to be hoarded. It *wanted* to be shared. Women and men wanted to feel it, to connect with someone who could reciprocate, and being part of Reed and Kate's dating challenge made them want more. For the first time Reed looked at the dating challenge from their perspective and saw the hope in their eyes. They wanted love and the challenge made them believe they could have it. But would the night end as he hoped?

Chapter 16

As Reed entered the balloon-filled house, Kate watched from down the street. Ember, Tanner, Marta, and Brittney were crowded around her at the corner of the fence, all laughing as the balloons poured from the front door and spilled onto the front lawn.

"There's so many," Kate said.

"You said a thousand," Tanner said, and then lifted his hands. "And my fingers still hurt."

"Mine too," Marta said.

"Worth it," Ember said. "But I really wish we would've had time to play in the balloons." They all looked to Ember in surprise, who shrugged. "Just because I have a temper doesn't mean I don't like balloons."

Kate grinned and turned back to watch Reed emerge with the large balloon. The pop sounded loud even to them, and then he read the note she'd written just that morning. His smile was brighter than the afternoon sun.

It was the first time she'd seen him since she'd left New York, and the sight sent desire pooling in her gut. How was it possible that he was more attractive than she remembered? The urge to walk up to him and plant a kiss on his lips was overwhelming, and she gripped the end of the fence to prevent herself from sprinting across the gap.

"I can't believe he came back," she murmured.

Marta was the only one to overhear. "He loves you. Did you really think he'd just work for a year?"

"Yes," Kate said. "That's what we decided."

Marta chuckled quietly. "No decision survives long against a powerful emotion. It's what drives us forward."

Kate noticed the sadness to her eyes and a burst of guilt replaced her thoughts of Reed. "Marta," she said. "I'm sorry I'm messing up your Valentine's Day."

"You're not," Marta said, offering a sad smile. "I don't have plans you could mess up."

Kate reached out and took her hand. "Exactly one year ago I felt the same thing you did. And that night I met Reed."

She shook her head. "I'm not going to find someone on Valentine's Day."

"That's what I thought," Kate said. "I promise, you'll find your own Reed."

"He's leaving," Tanner said urgently. "We need to get out of sight."

Kate cast a lingering look at Reed as he got back into his car. Then she retreated with the others to the cars and climbed into Ember's Jeep. As they drove home Kate turned to Marta and raised an eyebrow.

"Are your cousins ready?"

"As ready as they can be," she said. "We were just missing a few things from Reed's mom, but she sent me a link an hour ago. I forwarded it to my cousins and they are setting it up."

"And you still won't tell me what the pictures are for?"

"Nope," Marta said with a smile. "Shelby was clear. This was a surprise we're letting Reed keep."

"What about dinner?" Kate asked, twisting to look at Tanner.

"Done," he replied. "All taken care of."

A flutter of nervousness entered Kate's chest as she realized that the only thing that remained was getting ready for the date, and one very important phone call. A glance at the clock on her phone revealed it was three, with just three hours until she was to meet him.

"Time to get you ready," Brittney remarked, unknowingly mirroring Kate's thoughts.

"And we're running out of time," Ember said, pressing on the accelerator.

"Why?" Kate asked. "I just need to get dressed and—"

"You aren't wearing anything you own," Ember said flatly. "Or that we own, for that matter. On days like today, you need a new dress."

"We don't have time to shop *and* get ready," Kate said.

"We'll make time," Ember said.

Realizing they would not be dissuaded, Kate relented, and they hurried to a street with several stores. Foregoing the casual shopping, Ember drove straight to the formal wear shops, and for the next two hours they sprinted between stores, and Kate tried on dozens of dresses that her roommates refused.

After making an "incorrect" observation, Tanner was banished to the jeep, leaving Kate with the blondes. They had shopped together on countless occasions but this felt different, and several times Kate found herself gripped by an overwhelming gratitude.

Five stores and nineteen discarded dresses later, she exited the changing room with a sparkly black and green number that brought her roommates to their feet. Their smiles were all the answer she needed and she turned to the mirror to admire the view. The green drew out her eyes, while the shimmering black made her look regal.

"That dress was *made* for you," Brittney said, her voice awed.

"I wish I could see his face when he sees you," Marta said wistfully.

"You look awesome," Ember said. "But we only have an hour left."

Kate left the mirror behind but the image remained in her mind as she changed. The prospect of seeing Reed so soon sent bursts of fireworks into her gut and she struggled to focus. Just minutes after finding the dress they were out the door, dress in hand. Ember raced home with all the haste of a Nascar driver, and Kate sprinted into the house to get ready. She ducked into her room and pulled out her phone, checking the time. She swallowed as she prepared for the most difficult task of the day, and then called the institute in New York.

She'd called earlier to set up a time, and Dr. Dickson's secretary had given her a five minute window where he would be available. Nervous, she began to pace until the secretary transferred her to his office. Then he picked up.

"Ms Williams," he said. "I must say I'm surprised to hear from you, what with all the happenings going on in your life."

"I'm sorry if I'm interrupting," she hedged. "I know how important your time is—"

"Nonsense," he dismissed her worry. "I'm intrigued. Please tell me the purpose of your call."

Kate steeled herself for the request. Asking Reed to come back to Boulder was huge, and meant an enormous sacrifice. If this call went well, she might be able to soften that blow. If Dr. Dickson agreed.

"First I want to apologize," she said. "I know our relationship has made Reed's place in the institute a little tenuous."

"Indeed."

She winced at his tacit agreement and realized she was sweating. "I think you believe in Reed, and it's my hope that this request will not be out of place."

"We rarely receive without asking first," he said.

She forged ahead. "I wanted to ask if Reed could continue his internship from here in Boulder." He was silent for a moment and she forced herself to release a breath.

121

"Your request is highly unorthodox. Our interns learn a great deal from the personal interaction with the doctors here."

"I could fly him back once a month," she said. "And I know much of his work has been in performing research for dates. Reed could continue the bulk of that here. With me."

Dr. Dickson chuckled, the sound tinged with admiration. "Ms Williams, you are clever and bold. I can see why Reed is so attached."

Not an agreement, but Kate took it as hopeful. "I propose that Reed and I do research here, and he flies out to New York to finish said research and work with the other members of the institute. This would come at my expense, of course."

There was a creak on the phone, as if a chair was being leaned back. Dr. Dickson was probably still at work, sitting in his office as he pondered her request. He hadn't given an outright refusal, and she took that as a good sign.

"Your request puts me in a difficult position," he finally said. "Reed has shared a portion of his plans with me, and they might conflict with your offer. In addition, the institute is my first priority, not the interns. Do you understand?"

"I believe I do." Kate slowly sank onto her bed.

"Nevertheless," he said. "I will give you until tomorrow at noon. If he agrees to your plan, I may be able to work this out—with two weeks here, and two weeks in Boulder each month."

She leapt to her feet, and fought to keep her voice from betraying the burst of elation. "Thank you, Dr. Dickson."

"Before you celebrate," he said. "I should warn you that such a choice may not be necessary."

Confusion pierced her triumph. "What do you mean?"

"Just know that in every relationship, there comes a moment where a couple must decide to stay together, or break what has been built. I suspect that such a choice lies ahead for you tonight."

Kate stared at her sparkly dress, confused and now worried. What did Dr. Dickson know? What was Reed planning that would be in conflict with her idea? Discarding the seed of doubt, she realized that if such a choice came tonight, she could only hope that whatever happened on the date, they would stay together.

"I hope that choice is tonight," she finally said. "Because I want to be with Reed."

"That's what I like to hear," Dr. Dickson said. "Enjoy your evening, Ms. Williams."

Kate thanked him again and then hung up. Drawing in a long breath, she tried not to let the mystery get to her. One year ago she'd stood in the same spot, irritated at her roommates for setting her up with Reed. Now she was about to end the challenge. She just hoped he would say yes to her invitation.

After the fastest shower of her life, she sat in a chair while her roommates applied makeup and did her hair, their hands pulling, tugging, tying, and applying. When she opened her eyes thirty minutes later, she stared at the vision of beauty. She rose to her feet, her hands rising to her face.

Brittney had applied her characteristic light touch of makeup, just enough to bring out the natural beauty. Ember and Marta had curled her hair at the bottom, while tying back the top to leave two artful strands to frame her face. The rest fell in ringlets down her neck.

"Reed will be speechless," Ember said smugly.

Kate laughed and hugged her roommates, her gratitude welling into tears that Marta quickly condemned. Then she embraced her anyway. Brittney picked up the dress and they carefully threaded it over her shoulders. Kate wiggled in delight as the soft material flowed over her skin and fell to her legs. Then she turned and gave a final inspection.

"I can't believe you've done so much for me," Kate said.

"What else were we going to do?" Brittney asked, and then looked at the clock on her phone. "Which reminds me, I need to get ready."

"For what?" Marta asked, as all three turned to look at her.

123

"I have a date," Brittney said. She smirked and walked away, leaving the other three in the bathroom.

"When did that happen?" Marta asked.

Kate frowned. "You don't think that Reed . . ."

Ember scowled and stabbed a finger towards Brittney. "He bought you with a *date*?"

Brittney leaned back into view, her smile bright. "Worth it!" she sang.

Kate laughed and turned to the glowering Ember. "She's happy. I'm happy."

"I guess," Ember said reluctantly. "But we shouldn't have trusted her."

"I trust all three of you," Kate said. "Because you will always do what's best for me. And now it's my turn to do something for you."

Ember and Marta exchanged a look and Ember folded her arms. "What do you mean by that?" she asked cautiously.

"Ember," Kate said. "You've got thirty minutes before Tanner will be here to pick you up for dinner."

"But I told him I was helping you tonight," Ember said.

"And I relieve you of your obligation," Kate said with a smile.

Ember shook her head. "It's not really fair. With you all dressed up, you're impossible to refuse."

Kate grinned and turned to Marta. "And you need to get ready too."

Marta was watching Ember, her expression amused. At Kate's comment she blinked in surprise. "Me? I don't have a date."

"You do now," Kate said. "Thirty minutes from now your date will arrive, and you'd better be nice, because he's a good one."

Kate smiled and waited. Ember and Marta exchanged a look, an excitement threading into their own features. Then they scattered, and Kate retreated to her own room. She turned on the projector again and used the light to tie her heels and gather her purse. Then she picked up the phone and called Reed.

"Hello, beautiful," Reed said.

He sounded rushed and she heard the shower turn off. "How do you know I'm beautiful?" she asked.

"Because I tried to get my informant to send me a picture of your dress and she refused."

"Brittney?" she asked. "Well played. I assume you set her up with Caleb?"

"I did," he replied. "I've wanted to for weeks, but now was a good time."

"I'm glad you did," Kate said. "I would have hated the idea of her sitting home alone, but anyone I called already had plans. I did manage to take care of Ember and Marta, though."

"Who'd you set up with Marta?" Reed asked, his voice muffled as if he was putting on a shirt.

The doorbell rang and Kate swung the door open a crack. She peeked out and watched Marta open the door, to reveal Baker framed in the opening. He'd replaced his jeans and snug shirt for a button up and slacks, and Marta seemed momentarily stunned.

"You must be Marta," Baker said. "I'm Kate's brother."

Marta threw a look back and caught Kate watching. Marta's expression was dazed, her smile bright as she mouthed, *thank you!* Then she caught her purse and followed Baker from the house. Kate nodded her gratitude to Baker and he returned the gesture before shutting the door.

"Bake is taking her to dinner," Kate finally answered.

There was a pause on the other end of the line and then Reed's voice sounded closer. "That explains why he texted me to ask about a good place to take a girl to dinner."

"He asked you for dating advice?" Kate asked, her voice rising in astonishment.

"I guess he did," Reed said. "Now hurry up, or you're going to be late."

She grinned and glanced at the clock on the nightstand. "I think we already are."

"I had a lot to do today," he said. "But I'll see you in ten."

"Love you," she said.

"You too," he replied.

They hung up and Kate cradled the phone in her hand, her smile turning soft. How was it possible to feel so much for Reed? She wanted to be with him, not for a week or a year, but a lifetime. One year ago she'd felt a spark in her chest, and it had grown to a burning in her chest that had altered the very nature of hope.

She gathered her purse and looked about the room one final time. Since deciding to ask Reed her question she'd felt a lingering fear, but now that fear had been banished, cast aside by the bright hope that now blazed within her soul. In that moment she knew what his answer would be.

He would say yes.

Chapter 17

Reed left Jackson at his house and jumped into his old car. Then he pulled up the list of addresses on his phone that Caleb had prepared and rushed to the first. He didn't have time to check them all, so he watched the clock as he visited the houses.

The list had grown beyond what he would have thought, taking on a life of its own as if the entire city had joined his cause. The volunteers came from the team he'd met on the plane, old friends, girls he'd dated, friends from the program, and even Kate's friends. But there were many he did not know, their names and addresses unfamiliar to him. All knew him.

"Good luck tonight!"

"We'll be ready!"

"We'll see you tonight!"

The statements came from women and men, couples and even teenagers, all participants that had watched his challenge unfold and voted on the dates. Someone had passed out buttons that said, *We're with Kate*, or *We're with Reed*. He had no idea who had paid for the buttons but they were everywhere, with even the gas station attendant wearing one. The girl winked when he stopped to fill up the car.

"Have fun tonight, Reed."

"I will," he said.

He accepted the receipt and walked to his car, but waved when someone honked at him. The couple in the car waved at him like he was an old friend, but Reed had never seen them before. Shaking his head, he climbed into his car and pulled out his phone to call Kate.

"How's New York?" she teased.

"Great," he said, turning onto the road. "But everywhere I go, people seem to be involved in some big dating challenge."

"It's going on here too," she said. "Someone even printed buttons."

"I have no idea who did that," he said.

"Really?" she asked, her tone suspicious.

"Honest," he said. "It's a good idea, but I don't even have money for that right now. I'm all in for a big date tonight."

"I'm sure Hannah will love it," she said.

Reed laughed, and then noticed a car next to him with REED + KATE in the window. Written by hand, the message had been taped on the inside of the glass, the bold lettering bright with multiple colors. At the bottom was the link to Ember's blog.

The girls in the car noticed Reed and veritably exploded with excitement. They looked to be older teenagers from a local high school. Reed waved, sending them into fits before the light turned green and he pulled away.

"I'm beginning to feel like the challenge has gotten out of hand," he said ruefully.

"Wait, are we not pretending anymore?" she asked. "Because I'm *really* excited about tonight."

"You aren't the only one," he said, and told her about the car he'd seen.

"I saw our names on a billboard," she said. "Apparently they voted for you."

"The high school supports you," Reed said, slowing to read the message on the high school sign.

128

"I had a girl today tell me I needed to punch Hannah," Kate said with a laugh. "If a random girl knows about Hannah, it's gotten out of hand."

"Well at least it's over tonight," he said. "After that, we won't need the challenge anymore."

"What's that supposed to mean?" she asked, her tone cautious yet burning with curiosity, and a little worry?

"You'll find out soon enough," he replied.

She released an explosive breath. "Not soon enough. I'll see you soon."

"Love you," he said.

He heard her take a breath as if to steady her voice. "I love you, too," she said softly.

He hung up and then hurried home, arriving just before Jackson. Reed waited for his former roommate as he exited the car with Shelby. The two were dressed up for dinner and clearly running behind.

"You're late," they said in unison.

"I just need to shower and get dressed," Reed said. "Do you have the tux?"

Jackson held up the clothing bag. "Think it will fit?"

"It better," Reed said.

Shelby gauged the two of them as they walked inside. "You've got the same build, even if Jackson has an inch on you. It should."

"Thanks," Reed said, accepting the bag. "For everything. I really couldn't have done this without you."

"You helped him propose," Shelby said. "And even introduced us. Without you, we wouldn't have each other." She smiled at Jackson who inclined his head. "Have fun, but I expect a full report when you get back."

"Who says I'm sleeping here?" Reed asked.

Their eyes widened but Reed merely laughed and ducked into the bathroom. He took the fastest shower of his life and then dressed in Jackson's tux, left over from a wedding where he'd been one of the groomsmen.

As Shelby had predicted, it was a shade too long in the leg, but not enough to be noticeable. The shirt was white, the bow tie a nice black that complemented the tux. He slipped into the jacket and looked into the mirror.

He'd rented a tux for the benefit a few weeks ago, but this fit better. The jacket framed his shoulders and narrowed his waist, making him appear lean and muscular, handsome and engaging. He smiled, his blue eyes brightening with confidence.

"One last date," he murmured.

Jackson and Shelby had already left, so he entered the kitchen and loaded several items into a box. Candles, rose petals, a white tablecloth, and fine dishes. It took two trips to load them into his car and then he drove to the observatory. The bustle of the morning was gone, and only Lisa remained in the parking lot. He got out and picked up a box, while she grabbed the second and walked him inside.

"You're late," she said.

"I had a few things to check," Reed said, holding the door for her.

"Well you look great," she said.

Reed noticed the button on her shirt. *I'm with Reed.* "Where'd you get the button?"

"My roommate had a box of them," she said. "Said she got them at her work."

"I don't even know who paid for them," Reed said.

Lisa paused in reaching for the theater doors. "Does it matter? The world isn't a great place right now and you've shown others that romance isn't dead."

"Is that why you did so much for me?"

Lisa flashed a faint smile. "I did it to say thank you."

"For our date?" he asked. "That was years ago."

"For all the dates since," Lisa said. "Since you, I've been on a dozen creative dates, and my boyfriend does it too. You may not realize it, but you've started a trend, one that more and more guys are starting to follow."

"I didn't realize it had grown so much," Reed said, surprised and gratified by her words.

"It's not just your challenge anymore," she said.

She swung the door open to reveal the theater. He walked inside and turned around, marveling at the changes to the domed room, most of which had not been done by him. He looked to Lisa and found a smile on her face.

"Thank you," Reed said.

"Have a good time tonight," she said. "And don't worry about locking up. I plan on using the room after you're gone."

"Does your boyfriend know what's in store for him?"

Lisa laughed lightly. "He has no idea."

Lisa turned and left, leaving Reed in the room alone. With all the chairs and tables removed, the room was empty to the walls, the room illuminated only by the incredible vista displayed on the ceiling. Reed felt a chill cross his flesh and set his box down. Then he removed his jacket and went to work, laying out the final preparations.

Kate texted when she was on her way and he hurried to finish, dropping the last rose petal just as he heard a car door shut. Donning his jacket again, he jogged to his place and picked up a rose. Then he turned to the door and waited. Several seconds passed while he listened to his heart batter his ribs. Then the door swung open and Kate glided into the room.

Chapter 18

Kate got into her car and drove toward the observatory. Signs about the dating challenge seemed to have blossomed throughout the day, appearing on cars, billboards, and even the buttons Reed had spotted. She slowed to gawk at a sign that read, *Happy Valentine's Day, Reed and Kate!* The sign was outside a strip mall and usually advertised discount pizza. To see her name written in lights was surreal.

She pulled up to the observatory and Reed's former car. Even though he'd sold it to Roman, its presence sent a thrill of familiarity into her stomach. Reed had been gone for weeks, but right now he was here with her, and not even New York City was stronger than the bond they shared.

Her phone buzzed and she pulled it out, shocked to see dozens of missed calls and texts. Most were congratulatory and came from friends and family. There was even one from Aura, which was a surprise.

She smiled and messaged them back, and then put her phone away, not wanting a distraction from what she knew was coming. A chill swept across her skin as she got out of her car and picked her way up the sidewalk to the entrance. She stepped inside—and stared.

Candles dotted the room, casting the lobby in soft light. A sign on the coat stand, fashioned from wood and twine, invited her to leave her coat behind, so she removed her coat and hung it from a hook. Then she saw the floor.

Rose petals fluttered on the floor, drawing a line to the theater room, the sheer volume adding a sweet scent to the space. She smiled and shivered, but not from the chill, and then advanced toward the doors.

She caught the handle and swung the door open, sending a gust of warm air across her dress, ruffling the hem and scattering rose petals. She entered the auditorium and took in the room. More rose petals carpeted floor, growing thick as they approached the single table at the center of the room. Candles lined the walls, adding soft light to the domed theater and making the rose petals seem to dance.

The ceiling displayed the heavens, stars and constellations, comets, planets, and suns. The massive screen made the theater seem like it was floating among the stars, the dinner table joining the eternities.

Soft music played in the background, but she could not discern the source. The melody added to the ambience, inspiring comfort and awe in equal measure, yet the soft tones merely enhanced the figure that drew her gaze.

Reed stood adjacent to the table, his tux highlighting his frame, his shoulders slightly tilted, his hand in one pocket, pulling his jacket back to reveal lean hips. He held a single rose in the other hand, as if the flower had blossomed and coated the floor for her arrival.

Their eyes met and he smiled, his blue eyes startling even with the distance. Her breath caught and words abandoned her lips, her tongue going dry as she drank in his figure. As if of their own accord, her legs carried her forward, sending rose petals fluttering as she crossed the space.

Spellbound, she did not speak, could not speak. Reed was everything she'd ever wanted, yet so much more, and here he was, taking their date beyond the confines of the earth, like the love they shared could not be measured in earthly numbers.

She reached him and he placed the rose in the vase situated at the center of the table, the action hardly noticeable as her arms lifted to wrap around his neck. Reed too, seemed struck to silence, his arms snaking around her waist, his fingers tightening on the small of her back. Their bodies pressed together and she knew.

She would love him forever. No job, no distance, no amount of time could hold them apart. Even sex did not compare with the intimacy of their embrace, and she realized she finally understood why he'd wanted to wait. It wasn't because he did not desire her, it was because he desired more.

The roiling emotions in her heart swelled up and she raised herself on her toes, leaning into a kiss that began with a brushing of their lips, and quickly escalated, pumping to every last vestige of her skin until she felt like she could burst from heat and joy.

They parted and she struggled to find her center, and found it in his gaze. "I missed you," she murmured, her voice finally breaking the spell.

He reached up and brushed his fingers across her check. "Boulder or New York, you are my home."

She laughed lightly. "Then why did you ever leave?"

"I don't know," he said fervently. "But after tonight, I don't think we'll be apart again."

Her eyes widened and she struggled to comprehend the connotation of what he meant, her thoughts spinning in circles. He gave a small smile as if he knew exactly the impact his words conveyed, and then stepped back and gestured to the space at the side.

"Dinner isn't supposed to be here for a few minutes," he said. "Care to dance?"

Still struggling to comprehend what he'd meant, she inclined her head. "How can I refuse you in a tux?"

"You can't," he said, his lips twitching. "But do you *know* how beautiful you are? In that dress, you're captivating."

He caught her hand and spun, sending her into a twirl. Her dress fluttered, sending rose petals spinning across the carpet. She rotated back to him and he caught her hand, deftly turning her into a spin that brought them together.

"I do think you've outdone yourself," she said.

"It's not too much?" he asked, glancing to the roses on which they danced.

"No," she said with a smile. "It's breathtaking."

Her gaze lifted to the ceiling, which showed a comet streaking across the background, the giant ball of ice soaring in all its majesty. The sheer size of the screen made her feel like she'd left the earth behind.

"How did you pull this off in just a day?" she asked.

"I don't really know," he said, his voice mystified. "I asked for help and people just showed up, more and more until it had seemed to gain a life of its own."

"The rose petals are a nice touch," she said.

"It's our final date of the challenge," he said. "I had to make sure it was the best."

"I think you've done that," she said with a laugh.

"The night is young," he said cryptically.

"Will you stop that?" she exclaimed. "You're killing me with the innuendo."

He twirled her out and pulled her back in. "Sorry," he said. "I just know what's coming."

"Not all of it," she said.

He grunted, the sound a mixture of amusement and irritation. "I'm well aware you've managed to hijack my plans."

"As you said," she said, "It's the last date of the challenge. I had to make sure it was the best."

He pulled her and swung her towards a different section of the floor. "Do you remember a year ago?" he asked, and motioned to the floor. "This is the very spot we sat on our first date."

"Really?" she asked, and looked about herself.

True to his word, they were dancing on the same location where they'd sat on their first date. She recalled what she'd felt on that date, the uncertainty, the doubt. Now? She doubted she would recognize the person she'd become.

"Where were you two years ago?" she asked. "You know I was turning down Jason, but you never told me where you were."

"In my pajamas," he said. "I took the night off and hung out at my house. I think Jackson and I watched kung fu movies and talked about girls."

Kate smiled at the image. "Was he wearing his unicorn pajamas?"

"You know what? I think he was."

He spun her out and twirled her again, the motion recalling their dance at the swing hall on their second date, the one where she'd issued the challenge. For several moments they merely spun and danced, and she relished the moment, wishing it could go on forever.

A knock at the door interrupted her thoughts and they paused. "That must be dinner," he said.

"It is," she replied.

He frowned at her expression. "What did you do?"

"Changed our dinner plans," she said with a smile. "Stay here."

She leaned up to kiss him and then walked out of the theatre. When she reached the door she found Jackson and Shelby already inside with a package from a restaurant. Both were staring about the room in wonder.

"Rose petals?" Jackson exclaimed. "I didn't know about that."

"Thanks for grabbing dinner," Kate said.

"Happy to help," Shelby said, handing Kate the bag. "Have fun tonight."

"I will," Kate said.

She took the bag while Shelby dragged Jackson from the room. Then Kate carried it inside the theatre and to the table. The plates and dishes were already set, so she began to unload the food next to the plates, retrieving the bag with the bread last. The moment she opened it Reed smiled at the unmistakable scent.

"Is that what I think it is?" he asked.

"Yes it is," she replied with a smile.

Chapter 19

The moment Kate stepped out of the theatre, Reed darted to the door and peeked through the crack, watching her talk to Jackson and Shelby. He shook his head in amusement, not surprised that Jackson had helped.

He fleetingly wondered if Kate had known about the theatre, but her expression when she'd entered the room could not have been feigned. No, the ceiling, the rose petals, the dinner table, Kate hadn't known any of it, and her delight had been genuine.

Kate finished wrapping up the conversation and returned to the theatre. Reed darted to the table, arriving just as Kate opened the door. She smiled knowingly and crossed the room. He studied the package at her side but had nothing to indicate its source. All he knew was that it smelled Italian. Then she opened the bag with the bread.

"Is that what I think it is?" he asked.

"Yes it is," she said, her smile mischievous.

"Why Olive Garden?" he asked.

"You haven't figured it out?" she asked, turning and wrapping her arms around his neck. "It's the one date I wasn't with you."

He began to laugh as he recalled her date with Jason to Olive Garden, where Jason had said he was still in love with her. Now Kate was claiming that one night and giving it to him, a tacit admission that Jason was long gone.

"You're wonderful," he said.

"I'm hungry," she replied. "I was distracted today and didn't really get to eat."

He grinned and held her chair. Then he took his own seat. The soft music continued to play and the stars swirled in the ceiling above. He picked up a lighter and ignited the candles on the table, the burst of light illuminating her face.

"I really can't believe you did all this," she said, sweeping her hand at the room.

"I can't believe you did all this," he shot back, gesturing to the table.

She smiled. "You're really surprised?"

"I suspected you had taken over dinner," he said. "But I had no idea what you had planned. What about you? Did you know about the observatory?"

"Nothing," she admitted. "Sometimes I wonder who's really in charge. Us? Or our friends."

"Them," he replied with a wry smile. "They only told me what they thought I needed to know, not what *I* wanted to know."

"What else do you know about tonight?" she asked as she served her dinner.

"You first," he countered.

He opened the package for dinner and grinned. The meal was obviously the stuffed chicken marsala, his favorite, even though he hadn't had it for years. He served a piece to himself and then collected a portion from the salad container.

"How did you know it was my favorite?" he asked, indicating dinner.

"Aura, actually," she said.

"You called Aura?"

Kate pointed a teasing finger to him. "You're the one that said I should be friends with her. Besides, your mom and sister didn't know."

"We didn't go to Olive Garden often," Reed said. "But I'm still surprised you called Aura."

"You're dodging my question," she said.

"So are you," he replied with smirk.

She laughed and took a bite, and he took the time to consider just how much he wanted to tell her what he knew. It also depended on how much she knew. Then Kate took a sip of water and inclined her head.

"Cards on the table?"

"Deal," he said. "But no revealing what you did—just what you know about."

"Agreed," she said. "And I'll go first. I knew about dinner."

"I already knew that," he protested.

"You agreed to cards on the table," she said sweetly. "Your turn."

He laughed in chagrin and raised his glass to her. "I know you added pictures to our activity."

"I know you *needed* pictures for your activity," she countered.

His eyes narrowed. "Anything else about the activity?"

"Nothing," she said.

The irritation to her voice revealed that she'd tried to get more information—and failed. He smiled, grateful the knowledge about the projectors was safe. She glared at his expression and pointed her fork at his face.

"You don't need to look so smug."

"I'm just glad I've managed to keep a few secrets," he said. "But I'm impressed that you know so much."

141

"What's happening at the stadium?"

His heart stuttered in his chest but he kept his voice calm. "Why do you ask?"

"Just heard whispers of something happening at the stadium. Does it have to do with the projectors?"

Relief flooded his veins as he read the truth on her face. She didn't know, and was merely fishing for more, the banter as familiar now as it was a year ago in the same room. Only this time there was a lot riding on the secret.

"I think that's enough fishing," he said.

"Getting close to the truth?"

"Uncomfortably," he said wryly.

She smiled but let the matter drop. "What did you have planned for dinner tonight?"

"Something not as good," he said.

"As Olive Garden?" she asked, incredulous. "You always plan everything, so what was it?"

He hesitated, and then said, "Wendy's."

She snorted into her water. "You were bringing fast food . . . to this?" she swept her hand at the theater."

He nodded, a sly smile playing across his features. "It was what Jackson and I ate in Florida."

"On the date I missed," she said.

Her eyes widened as she recognized the truth, he'd planned the dinner for the exact reason she had, to share a piece of the dating challenge that had not been for the other. Then she began to laugh, the sound echoing off the celestial ceiling.

"You get points for the thought," she said. "But this is better."

"We do *everything* better together," he replied. "Including date."

"You mean that?" she asked, her amusement fading. "I did steal portions of your date."

"You added to it," he replied.

"I must admit I'll be sad to see this challenge go," she said. "I've gotten used to looking forward to the next date."

"The challenge may end, but we're not going to stop," he replied.

"I know," she said, and then flashed a mischievous smile. "Especially after tonight."

He shot her a look, but it was obvious she wasn't talking about his plans. She had her own. He cocked his head to the side, wondering what else she had up her sleeve. Again he felt a tremor of trepidation, and wondered what he would do if her plan contrasted with his. Before he could ask, she changed the subject to their events of the last year.

Throughout the meal they spoke softly. Every once in a while he caught a whiff of roses and smiled, his eyes lifting to the screen above. It was so large that the entire room seemed to have left the earth. The flickering of candles added to the sense of movement, and Reed found a rare sense of pride swelling in his chest.

"You're pretty proud of yourself, aren't you?"

Caught, he grinned. "If I admit the truth, I've thought about this date for ages, but knew I had to save it for someone special."

"You should be proud," she said. "But don't get cocky on me. This doesn't mean you've won."

"We'll see," he said, wiping his napkin on his lips.

They'd finished the meal, or as much as they were going to eat of the traditionally large Olive Garden portions. They boxed up the leftovers and he took them into the fridge in the employee lounge. Then he returned and cleared the dishes, which he left in the sink of the break room. When he returned he found her staring at the ceiling.

"Do we have to leave?"

"Not yet," he said.

She sighed, the sound wistful. "Can we dance again?"

He answered by taking her hand and pulling her in. This time they did not talk, and she merely placed her head on his shoulder. He turned her slow, swaying with the music as they danced under the stars.

As they drifted across the carpet of rose petals, he marveled at the contrast, of how public their challenge had become, yet how intimate their relationship truly was. He didn't mind the thousands that wanted to be part of the challenge, but none had seen what he saw now. Kate, in all her beauty and courage, dancing with him where none could see. They circled for several minutes, their bodies close, and she felt her heart beat against his chest. It could have lasted for hours and he would never have wanted to leave.

"Promise me we'll do this again," she said.

"The next time the stars won't be in a theater," he replied.

"I'll hold you to that," she said, retreating a step and blinking like she was waking from a dream. "Do we need to blow out the candles?"

"Nope," he said. "Lisa, the manager who let me do this, asked if I could leave them for her and her boyfriend."

They shared a last look at the empty room, at the white table now empty, and the scattered rose petals. Then she nodded and hooked her arm into his, allowing them to walk to the door. She collected her coat on the way out and they braved the blast of cold air to reach his car. As they did, the third car in the parking lot came to life and came forward.

Reed spotted Lisa in the front seat and gestured an invitation to the building. Then he helped Kate into the car and circled to get into the driver's seat. As he backed out of the lot she pointed toward the stadium.

"To the stadium?" she asked. "I'm excited to see the pictures."

"Nope," he replied. "The pictures aren't in the stadium, they're on the way there . . ."

Chapter 20

Kate frowned in confusion. She'd heard whispers of the stadium, overheard in hushed conversations between her roommates, and assumed that was where the pictures would be needed. Maybe displayed on the stands? But no, it wasn't there. He drove down the street and pointed to the dash clock, which was just turning to 7:30.

"Ready?"

"For what?" she asked.

Reed's smile was contagious. "Just watch."

They drove down the street, roughly headed to campus. Then she noticed groups of people outside their homes, standing on their driveways and talking. They were on both sides of the street and all over, and she was about to ask what they were doing. Then the clock changed to 7:30 and the groups went into action.

A projector glowed to life and shone on the garage door, the image that of Kate's first date with Reed. They sat together, Reed at a discreet distance, the background revealing the mountains where they'd had their dinner. Their smiles were casual, comfortable, the expressions of friendship without knowing what lay in store.

Across the street was another picture from the same night, a candid taken by her roommates after she returned home. Kate's smile was soft, as if she was remembering a moment from the date. Since Brittney and Marta were in the picture it could have only been taken by Ember. Then a house down the street lit up. And the next.

Then suddenly they were everywhere.

She gasped as images of the past year blossomed on all sides, pictures from their challenge dates, selfies taken between dates, and pictures of the two of them together. The images were displayed on garages and walls, even once on the side of a van. There were so many the whole city seemed to brighten.

There were pictures of the St. Patrick's Date, their bodies painted in color. The next showed them dressed in Hogwarts clothing. The date where they'd driven the go karts and when they'd been stranded on the road. The date with the fireworks where she'd thought their relationship was over, and the date with the lanterns, when she knew they were together.

Tears formed in her eyes at the flood of memories, of all the moments that now culminated in this, the final date. The people who'd set up the projectors began to cheer, shouting and clapping as Reed and Kate drove by. Tens became hundreds, all with projectors showing the dating challenge.

"How did you do this?" she breathed, her words barely above a whisper.

"Word spread," he replied. "And people just kept wanting to help."

She glanced his way and saw that he too, was moved, his expression shocked and grateful. Her hand found his and she smiled, attempting to convey in a single look what the incredible display meant to her.

And still the pictures were there, showing him sleeping on the air mattress on her floor during the marathon date, and then a picture of her at the cabin for the Christmas Date. The one with Reed and Kate's brothers, with him standing in the center, drew a burst of laughter.

As they drove through the streets of Boulder the images gradually changed, showing not just their dates, but other pictures taken between the challenge dates, of the year they had spent together. Pictures of her texting on her phone, obviously taken by one of her roommates, the caption making it clear she was talking to Reed. Others showed Reed at school, his notebook showing date ideas, some of which he'd used. The next revealed the calendar from Reed's wall, two dates with Kate clearly marked.

She wrestled to contain the rising emotion but it swept her under as she bore witness to attraction that had grown to love. She caught glimpses of him in settings she'd never seen, and saw scenes of herself, taken by others, that showed her falling in love.

"What's that?" Reed asked, pointing to one picture on a garage door.

Kate smiled as the picture showed Reed as a child, his dark hair messy, his blue eyes sparkling with mischief. The next showed Kate, also as a child, her brown hair in pigtails, her dress dirty from wrestling in the mud with one of her brothers.

"You added these?" he asked.

She nodded, unable to speak. She'd thought to add pictures of their time before, but merged into the cascade of memories from the last year they gained a different connotation, like they'd spent their entire lives waiting to be together, and the moment they had, their destiny had been assured.

She glanced at Reed but his eyes were on the sea of images, each house leading to another, more and more people standing next to projectors and even televisions that had been hauled onto the driveways.

They went up and down nearly empty roads, reliving the dating challenge through a hundred separate scenes, the snapshots merging into a single, massive demonstration of how they'd fallen in love.

Not all the pictures were perfect, with some depicting her date with Jason, another showing Reed sitting with Aura when she was in a coma, obviously taken by Jackson. The next one showed Kate hugging Aura on her lawn.

"I can't believe you did all this," she said.

"They get the credit," Reed said, waving to a large group of teenage girls that screamed as they passed.

"Still," she said. "You imagined it and it came together."

"I imagined a few streets and a dozen projectors," he said ruefully. "This feels like the entire city is part of our date."

The wonder in his voice matched her own sentiment, and she was again overwhelmed with all of the scenes from the last year. She craned her neck to see them all, and noticed other cars were lining up behind them, many leaning out windows, pointing and laughing at the projectors. She marveled at just how large the challenge had become.

They turned a corner and stared up her street, passing their house where Marta and Baker stood next to a tiny projector. The image was on their front door, and showed Kate and Reed locked in a kiss, right where they'd always said goodbye. Marta waved, and Reed waved back.

"It looks like they're getting along," Reed said.

Kate noticed they were holding hands, and Baker's expression was abnormally light, his normally forbidding expression almost happy. She'd only ever seen that expression when he had a gun in his hands.

"Two years ago I was crying on that porch," she said. "Now I see a picture of us kissing, and see my brother holding hands with my roommate."

"Took us a while to reach the kissing stage," he said wryly. "But it was worth the wait."

"Very," she said fervently, eliciting a smile.

Her phone buzzed and she pulled it out, her smile widening as she saw it was from Marta. "Turn left," she said.

"There's more projectors to the right . . ." He noticed her expression and his eyes narrowed. "What do you have planned?"

"Turn left and find out," she said.

He obliged and turned left, heading up the street two down from his former house. His expression of confusion turned to shock when he saw the first image, and tears formed in his eyes . . .

Chapter 21

Words failed Reed as he recognized the first pictures of Jackson and Shelby, of them standing together, their hands intertwined. Jackson and Shelby stood behind the image dressed for their own Valentine's date, waving at Reed as he passed. Under the image was a single phrase.

#CreativeDating

The next picture was of Melissa, the girl they'd met on the fireworks date. She stood with her fiancé, a ring on her hand, a smile on her face. The caption at the base of the image said the same, as did the next picture.

Again and again the pictures came, each showing couples that had come together because of creative dating. He recognized girls he'd taken on dates and guys that had followed his example. All with a companion. Overcome with emotion, he waved to the couples that had come together, who credited him for bringing them together.

Many were dressed up, either returning from or going to their own Valentine's dates. In suits and dresses, they smiled and waved to Reed as he slowly drove by, the pictures on the houses a backdrop of his legacy.

"I can't believe you did this," he breathed.

"I can't take the credit," she said. "It was Jackson's idea."

"Jackson thought of this?" Reed asked, sparing her a glance.

"He wanted you to know what you'd done for him, and once he posted it on Ember's blog it kind of snowballed. Of course, my roommates refused to let me look at the blog, so I suspect you posted on there something I shouldn't know . . ."

Reed swept a hand to the rows of displays. "I don't know what to say."

"This is your legacy, Reed," Kate said, the smile evident in her voice.

Reed then spotted Dr. Caldin. The professor stood outside a small home, his arm around his wife, his three teenage daughters standing with him. Bundled up in coats, they waved as Reed drove by. Their eyes met, and Dr. Caldin inclined his head, a slight smile on his face. The picture projected on the garage was of Dr. Caldin and his wife, skydiving.

Tears formed in his eyes as Reed understood. The promise he'd made to Aura, made out of regret, had quietly spread to others, even his professor, who'd used Reed's methods to date his wife. The way his daughters waved showed they knew Reed, indicating Dr. Caldin had passed on the instruction to his daughters.

"I never thought people would do this," Reed said softly, turning the corner to go up the next street.

"People want to find love," she said. "And you showed them how. You showed *me* how."

"*You* showed me how," Reed said, looking to her. "Before you I was going through the motions, but it was manufactured, a façade to hide my regret. Everything changed when you showed up. I knew how to date. You taught me how to love."

"I think that's a lesson that we learned together," Kate said, squeezing his hand.

They turned back to the parade of memories and Reed watched them go by, struck by how much Kate had done for him—even on a night he'd planned for her. He recalled thinking that he had the advantage in the dating challenge, but Kate had proven to be more than a competitor. She'd proven to be his equal.

151

They drove up a second street and then another, still there were houses with projectors and pictures. He'd hoped to set up a few dozen at best but there were hundreds, and so many people he did not know. He even spotted the girls he'd met on the airplane, who had driven up to Boulder to be part of evening. They waved and screamed as he went by, prompting Kate to ask who they were.

"I met them on the flight last night," Reed said, honking and waving. "They agreed to help spread the word."

"Which they certainly did!" she said with a laugh.

The parade of pictures finally ended on the street to the stadium and he slowed at the last house. Caleb stood outside his apartment, a "borrowed" school projector plastering a final picture of Reed and Kate on the wall. Caleb stood with Brittney, but apparently they'd grown tired of waiting.

"Are they . . .?"

Kate began to laugh. "Kissing. And yes, they are."

Reed honked and they parted. Brittney flushed and smiled while Caleb merely grinned and waved. Reed tipped an imaginary hat, both in gratitude for his friend's help, and to praise his forwardness.

"Well done, Brittney," Kate said, her tone filled with admiration.

Reed glanced back at the city, which seemed brighter than normal, all the houses around campus blazing with light from the hundreds of projectors. As he watched they began to go dark, turning off as the volunteers finished their part.

A chill swept across his skin as his thoughts turned ahead, to what he was about to do. Asking Kate to come to New York City was a big invitation, and he had no idea how she would respond. But that was not all he had planned, and there was one thing he hadn't told anyone. Not even Jackson. He swallowed the surge of nervousness and turned the car towards the stadium.

Kate seemed to notice where they were heading and raised an eyebrow. "We're almost to the stadium."

Reed pulled off onto the side of the road and turned to her. "Do you trust me?"

"Of course."

Reed reached into the backseat and retrieved a blindfold. "You once asked me to fall for you. Now I ask you to do the same."

She grinned and wrapped it around her eyes. "I'm pretty sure I already did that."

He smiled. "That's what I'm counting on . . ."

Chapter 22

Kate donned the blindfold and reached for Reed. The date had already surpassed anything she could have hoped for, so she had no idea what to expect at the stadium. But her heart battered in her chest, an engine fueled by nervousness and excitement.

Of all the places to go, why the stadium? And why was she blindfolded? The questions burned in her mind, each carrying more weight after the events of the date. Everything he'd planned, everything he'd implied, all suggested tonight was big. But how big?

It was probably just Reed being Reed, and today was just him wanting to finish the dating challenge as only he could. But it felt like more. A lot more. What more did he have up his sleeve?

She wiped her hands on her dress, a nervous motion that failed to smooth the electricity arcing beneath the surface. Just as she thought she would explode, Reed turned the music up.

"What's with the music?" she asked, grateful the inner turmoil did not show in her voice. "What don't you want me to hear?"

"This and that," he replied.

She heard the smile in his voice, but also a slight tremor. Was he nervous as well? Or was he just feeling the lingering impact from the parade of memories? She swallowed but her mouth was dry, and she tried to keep her voice even.

"More this?" she asked. "Or more that?"

"Definitely more that," he replied.

The car bounced over a gutter as it pulled into the stadium parking lot, and she mentally followed him through the turns. Even in an empty parking lot, he did not drive over the parking spaces, and followed the road to the front of the building.

He parked and got out, and she waited what seemed like forever for him to open the door, her nervousness mounting like a rocket attempting to breach the atmosphere. Then her door opened and he caught her hand, helping her to her feet.

"Stay with me," he said.

"Always," she replied with a light laugh.

He guided her to the building and warned her when to step up. She stumbled a little but managed to keep her feet, laughing as she righted herself and followed him toward the stadium. She'd wondered if it was all a trick and he had another destination in mind, but she could hear the wind under the bleachers, the sound reminding her of their second date, when she'd issued the challenge.

"Is there a blanket on the fifty yard line?" she asked.

He laughed. "I can't let you take advantage of me," he said.

She heard faint music and craned her ears to listen. "What's that?"

"We had music at the observatory," he said. "It's only fitting we have it here."

She smiled as she heard the romantic music, and realized he was using the entire stadium to set the mood. She wondered if he intended to drop his physical boundaries, her gut clenching at the prospect. But Reed would not do that here, not in the stadium. So why bring her here? And what was she not supposed to see?

"Watch your step," he said.

"I can't *watch* my step," she said.

He snorted a laugh and pulled on her arm. "The stairs are here."

"This isn't the main entrance," she said.

"That one is currently blocked," he said evasively.

155

She slowed and used her foot to feel forward. When she felt the concrete, she began to ascend, grateful Reed was at her side, holding her hand and elbow as they climbed into the bleachers. He caught her other hand and moved it to the railing, the cold metal grounding her and making her more stable.

"In the bleachers or on the field?" she asked.

"The field," he said.

A moment later they reached a short flight of stairs that dropped them to the track, and then he led her onto the grass. There was no snow on the field but the grass was cold, the green strands brushing against her toes, and causing her to shiver.

"We're almost there," he said.

"Are you nervous?" she asked.

"Maybe," he said with a chuckle.

"Should I be nervous?"

"Probably not," he replied.

"Probably isn't very comforting."

He laughed but didn't respond, and then slowed her and warned of another two steps. They'd only walked halfway across the field, and it felt like wood rather than concrete. Confused, she eased herself up the steps and came to a stop when he pulled on her hand. She heard him take a breath and her nervousness spiked.

"Reed . . .?"

He caught her shoulders and repositioned her. Then he spoke softly. "You can remove the blindfold."

She reached up and removed the dark cloth, blinking as her eyes refocused on Reed. They stood on a small stage at the center of the field. Shrouded in darkness, the bleachers were barely visible, the moonless night failing to illuminate the massive edifice. The stars twinkled in the sky, a reminder of their otherworldly dinner.

"Kate," Reed said, his voice soft. "Are you ready to finish the challenge?"

A chill swept across her that had nothing to do with the temperature. "I think so," she said.

Reed held her gaze, his easy smile on his face. Only this time there was an aura of anticipation about his features, as if he hid a giant secret he couldn't wait to share. She swallowed, afraid and yet excited beyond measure for this, the final surprise.

Reed drew in a breath as if to center himself and then spoke softly. "These weeks apart have been miserable," he said. "And I don't want us to be apart."

"And?" she asked. "We can't do anything about that." What was he getting at? Did he know her plan?

"Perhaps we can," he said.

She swallowed, wondering what he was getting at. "Reed, I can explain . . ."

"I want you to come to New York with me."

"What?"

She hadn't prepared for that, and the question landed heavy. They'd talked about it before, and knew there was no way they could. Confusion brought on silence, and he interpreted that as an invitation to continue.

"I found a place for you to stay in New York just a few blocks from me, with Dr. Dickson's niece. He also said he could help you get into NYU."

Stunned by his suggestion, she stared at him, the prospect of going to New York—permanently—spinning in her thoughts like a wheel in mud. But what about her plan? Did she want to stay in Boulder? Or go to New York?

"When?" she hedged, unwilling to share her own plan.

"At the end of the semester," he said. "Or . . ."

"Or what?" she asked.

"Or this weekend," he said. "You'd lose a semester, but we'd be in New York, together."

The weight he'd shouldered was suddenly hers, and she realized now what he'd been planning. He'd found a way for her to come and be with him, to continue her own education in a different university. It was a choice, to leave behind her life . . . and merge her life with his.

She'd wanted Reed to come to Boulder, but not because it was the best idea. It was her only hope to be with him, to not watch him leave again. Unknowingly, Reed had come up with his own solution to the same problem.

She envisioned her life unfolding, of her leaving the blondes, of taking a semester off and spending nights with Reed, of exploring New York City with him. He'd said she could wait until the end of the semester but she knew her answer . . .

"You don't have to choose right now," he said, a frown creasing his forehead at her silence. "I know it's a lot to take in . . ."

"I'm coming," she said firmly.

She thought of the question she'd come prepared to ask, and decided it didn't matter anymore. His invitation allowed them both to pursue their careers without requiring Reed to sacrifice. He'd found a way to shatter time, so nothing could pull them apart.

"Really?" His eyes widened with hope. "Are you sure?"

"This is what I want," she replied. "I want you."

"You can wait until the end of the semester . . ."

"No," she said, nodding her head. "This weekend. Now."

She smiled, the prospect of leaving with Reed finally settling in. Her semester apart—her year apart—suddenly fell away, relinquishing it's wealth of worry and misery to be replaced with adventure and excitement, of time with the one she loved.

She leaned up and kissed him, all the emotions of the last few hours distilling into a single powerful contact. Her hands clung to his neck, his to her back, binding them together the way they would remain.

When they parted Reed had the biggest smile she'd ever seen. "Then there's just one more thing to resolve. The challenge."

"And how do we resolve that?" she asked, her head still spinning from the kiss and the sudden change of her future.

Reed stooped and picked up an object at the edge of the platform. When he stood she recognized it as a microphone. She blinked in surprise but he brought it to his lips and spoke, his voice filling the stadium.

"Jackson?" Reed called. "Lights please."

The stadium lights glowed to life, gradually brightening to reveal the arena. Kate's confusion gave way to awe as she turned a slow circle, her eyes sweeping the bleachers as she realized the truth.

The stadium wasn't empty . . .

Chapter 23

Thousands of people—*tens* of thousands—were in the stands. They rose to their feet as the lights brightened, showing the massive crowd that had come to see the end of the final date. Kate's breath caught as she recognized her roommates in the front row, Brittney standing with Caleb, Marta with Baker, and Ember with Tanner. Jackson and Shelby were also there, as were so many others.

Students, faculty from the university, teenagers and adults, they were all there. Kate recognized many from the group that had set up the projectors, and thousands more. There were so many that she could scarcely imagine how they had come, just to see Reed and Kate.

She spotted the school marching band that had helped her do the invite for the Dare Date, and dozens from her engineering classes that had helped Reed do the invite for the Crazy Date. And still there were more.

Reed's neighbor that had loaned them the use of his pool for the Island Date, Reed's friend that had been there for the ill-fated Fireworks Date. Tanner and Tanner's brothers, Marta and Marta's mother, who seemed to be crying. Ramon and Marta's other cousins who had helped with the frozen rose.

She spotted Melissa and her fiancé, as well as Harold and his wife, who waved while he seemed out of place dressed in his overalls. Anna from the miniature golf course and Dr. Caldin with his wife and daughters. More and more, so many she could not see to name them all.

Families and children, teachers and couples, all gathered on the bleachers, filing into the stands, and still there were more. The stadium built to support over fifty thousand was half full, the crowd rising up the bleachers.

"Where did they come from?" she breathed.

Reed shrugged helplessly as if to say, *I never thought there would be this many.* She realized he'd invited everyone, and much like the parade of memories, it had spread far beyond his initial design. Then he put the microphone to his lips, his voice booming over the stadium.

"I'd like to thank you all for joining us for this moment," he said, his voice reverberating as if he were an announcer at real game. "I know you're all excited to give your vote on who has won this dating challenge, but there are a few people we'd like to thank."

"HE'S TALKING ABOUT ME!"

Jackson's bellow caused a ripple of laughter that cascaded across the crowd, with many calling out his name. Jackson stood proudly, his fists on his waist like he was a superhero. Shelby was laughing at his side.

"Our roommates," Reed said. "Jackson, Ember, Brittney, and Marta. From the beginning they were our spies and allies, and they were far more devious I ever thought possible."

Applause answered his words and mounted, with much stomping of feet and whistles. Jackson and the others stood and bowed, with much shoving between Ember and Jackson for the central focus. Laughter ensued, engulfing the crowd anew.

Kate watched in shock, still struggling to come to terms with how many had shown up, just to witness a winner of their dating challenge. She'd known it had gone public, but never in her wildest imaginations would she have thought so many were following Ember's blog.

"We also have to thank those who joined early in the competition," Reed said. "Shelby, Jackson's fiancé, our parents and siblings, who were surprisingly willing to betray us for our opponents."

More whistles and applause, the sound building as they all sensed the approaching moment, when the spectators would choose the winner.

She saw camera flashes and phones out, and she guessed it was streaming live, allowing thousands more to feel like part of the event.

She was abruptly aware of just how many eyes were upon her, and a light flush climbed up her skin. Reed glanced her way and reached for her hand, a smile and a nod reassuring her as he quickly listed others who'd helped from the beginning. When he was finished a palpable tension seeped into the air.

"Thank you to all those who have helped us in the challenge," Reed finished. "There is no way we could name them all, but you have to know, that without you . . . I wouldn't have won Kate."

Emotion clogged Reed's throat. He struggled to speak, to voice the gratitude for so many. Emotion welled up in Kate's chest but she snatched the microphone from his hands and turned to the crowd.

"Don't let that sway you," she called. "We all know that *I'm* the winner of the challenge!"

Laughter and shouts of agreement came from guys and girls, and those holding Kate buttons were quick to lift them high. A grin on his face, Reed accepted the microphone back and pointed to the booth at the top of the stadium.

"Last of all I'd like to thank the administration," he called. "They've put up with our antics across campus, and graciously loaned me the stadium—as long as I gave a promise that this would be the end of the challenge!"

Again laughter erupted and there was a growing applause. The scoreboard lit up in response, and a decibel counter appeared. In the time honored tradition, the people would decide who had won the dating challenge, by volume.

"Ladies first!" Reed said, offering the microphone to her.

She accepted it with a bow and turned to the audience, suddenly aware of just how many were there to support her. A nervous smile spread on her face and she raised her hand to the scoreboard.

"For all those who know I won, *let's hear some noise!*"

The stands erupted in cheering and stomping feet. Screams and whistles added to the cacophony, the sheer volume rising to a pitch that seemed to shake the stadium. The numbers on the scoreboard rocketed into the nineties and continued before slowing, and then came to a halt.

"104.9!" Kate roared, her voice hardly audible over the crowd.

Reed took the microphone and stepped to the front of the stage. "Well played," he called as the last people went quiet. "You put up a good fight, but I think we all know who *really* won this challenge . . ."

The roar that followed blasted the air, the screams and shouts reverberating off the bleachers as men and women stomped their feet. Kate heard girls screaming, the screams adding a high note to the stomping off the feet, and she held her breath as the numbers climbed to 103 . . . 104 . . . and then climbed beyond to 108.2.

She groaned as the crowd surged, the voices bellowing their victory and the Kate supporters shouting their dismay, inadvertently pushing the number even higher. Reed swept his hands in triumph and then brought the microphone to his lips.

"The crowd has spoken!" he roared.

The applause was thunderous from both sides as Kate pushed him on the side, feigning anger at the loss. Reed laughed as he basked in the victory, of the final triumph that could not be disputed. Kate looked on, shaking her head in amusement.

The noise finally subsided, allowing Jackson's voice to pierce the din. "WHAT DID YOU WIN?"

Reed held up the microphone. "Isn't it obvious?"

He wrapped his arms around Kate, pulling her into a kiss. Whistles and shouts again erupted, and thunderous applause swept the arena. Swept up in the moment, Kate knew she'd lost the challenge, but she'd won far more. When they parted his eyes were on her, the soft blue sparkling.

"I love you," he whispered.

"I love you," she said.

He smiled the same easy smile he'd always had, only now she noticed it had softened, a twist reserved just for her, the permanent mark he would have every time he looked at her. He stepped back and raised the microphone to his lips.

"Thank you all for coming," he said. "But before you go, there is one last thing I'd like to do."

He handed the microphone to Kate. Confused, she glanced to the crowd but they too seemed surprised, and some had just started toward the exit. Reed's request brought them to a halt as he reached into his pocket and pulled out an object. Then he smiled,

And went down on one knee . . .

Chapter 24

Kate's breath caught, her hand flying to her lips, and the decibel counter dropped to zero. Time seemed to freeze as all eyes focused on the object in Reed's hand. He looked up at Kate and raised a shining object to her, a diamond ring.

"Kate Williams," he said, his words barely heard through the microphone clutched in her hands. "Will you marry me . . .?"

The moment seemed frozen in time, her emotions—still chaotic from the last several minutes—grappled with what was happening. Reed's gaze was filled with hope and love, yet also the ultimate vulnerability.

She saw her life unfold with him, of a lifetime of dating, of children, of home. Of Reed at her brothers' houses and she and Natalie talking about their kids. It was a life she wanted, craved, loved.

But was she ready?

An image flashed across her mind, of Jason down on his knee—two years ago, today. On that day, a part of her had burgeoned to her lips and refused. This time, that same fire swelled in her chest, burning into every extremity—not with defiance—but with joy.

"Yes," she said.

The word slipped from her lips, momentarily filling the stadium. Tears filled her eyes and a smile blossomed on her face. A shout rang out, and like a gunshot at a race, it unleashed the frozen crowd, the roar gradually building, the sound topping 110 decibels unnoticed. The mic fell from Kate's hands and bounced off her shoe, sending a *cough* from the impact.

Reed came to his feet and swept her into a spinning embrace, her flowing dress spinning about the stage, her arms around the one she loved, the one she would be with forever. The one she'd won.

The happiness seemed to shatter her body, envelop and expand every facet of her soul. Moisture leaked from her eyes and she found herself shouting, screaming, the sound ending when his lips came to hers. He finally set her down, the bruising kiss relinquishing to a soft contact.

When they parted Reed held her gaze and slid the ring onto her finger. She had no idea how he'd gotten the size right, but it was Reed, so it was perfect. She wondered how long he'd been planning to propose, but decided it didn't matter anymore.

The challenge was over.

Her life had just begun.

Chapter 25

After the proposal Reed led Kate to the edge of the stadium where they hugged thousands as they exited the stadium. He felt like he was floating, like his feet were not on the ground. But his hand remained firmly in Kate's, their fingers intertwined. He hugged friends new and old, still surprised by the sheer volume of people that had come.

"Congratulations!" he heard for the hundredth time.

The crowd finally slowed to a trickle, and Reed spotted Jackson and Tanner picking up the pieces of the stage, using a cart to take them back into the tunnel. Administration officials descended from the booth, including the head coach of the Buffalos, who paused to shake their hands.

"Well played," he said, nodding to Reed before turning to Kate.

"Congrats to you both."

Then he reached out and caught his wife's hand before departing. Others wished their final farewell as Reed rode the last wave outside the stadium. As the last stragglers departed, Reed turned to his friends who had remained behind.

"I can't *believe* you didn't tell me about the ring," Jackson said, hitting him on the shoulder.

"Sorry," Reed said with a laugh. "But I only told one person."

"Who?" Kate asked.

Reed motioned to Baker, who stood next to Marta. He towered over the rest of the group but the proximity to Marta suggested a budding affection. He gave a faint smile as the group looked to him.

"He did ask permission," he said, almost apologetically.

"And you said yes?" Kate asked.

"I had to," he said with a shrug. "If I didn't, Ember would break my legs."

The ensuing laughter echoed off the walls of the stadium and the group stepped forward to embrace Reed and Kate. Baker even shook Reed's hand, an act that both surprised him, and nearly broke his fingers.

"This doesn't mean that I like you," he said to Reed.

"Yes it does," Reed said.

Baker grunted, a ghost of a smile appearing on his face before he walked with Marta toward his car. After giving their congratulations, the others departed as well, all to their own Valentine's celebrations. Reed watched them go, his heart filled with gratitude. When he finally turned to Kate he found her expression pensive.

"How long were you planning to do that?" she asked. "Because I know you didn't get the ring today." She held it up and admired the stone.

"I've had it for years," he admitted. "It was my grandmothers. She said I reminded her of my grandfather, so she wanted me to use it when I was going to get married."

"It's beautiful," she said.

"Do you really like it?" he asked.

They'd started walking to the car, the dropping temperatures finally sapping the euphoria of the last half hour. He watched her examine the ring again. A full karat diamond was bracketed by two emeralds in white gold, the stones shining in the lights of the parking lot.

"I couldn't have picked a better one for myself," she said.

He brought her to a halt next to the car, a touch of uncertainty rising in his chest. "I know I asked in front of everyone," he said. "So if you don't want—"

"I'll just stop you right there," she said. "Today when Bake showed up at my door, I asked him for my own permission."

"To do what?"

"I was going to ask you to come to Boulder."

"You were going to ask *me?*"

"I actually called Dr. Dickson." She told him about the conversation and her request.

He'd thought himself clever, but she had figured out her own plan, one that solved the very same problem. And she'd gone to great lengths to make sure it was possible, even convincing Dr. Dickson of what he'd thought would be impossible. Mistaking his silence, Kate's expression turned worried.

"Are you upset about coming to New York?" he asked.

"We're engaged," she laughed at the absurd question. "This is the best day of my life, but the prospect of a future with you? Either here or in New York, I'm just glad we don't have to be apart."

"That's how I feel," he said. "So New York or Boulder? Which do you want?"

She cocked her head to the side and he waited for the answer. Then she pointed east. "New York. We've finished one adventure. I'm ready for what comes next."

"You sure?"

"I've never been more sure about anything," Kate said, closing the gap. "Come what may, I want you."

"Even without the challenge?"

169

Her tinkling laugh sent a thrill into his stomach. "Reed," she said. "Haven't you realized the truth? The challenge was never about how you plan the date. The challenge was to see who could *be* the better date."

"Is that so," he said, sweeping her into his arms and lowering his voice. "Don't tell anyone, but I think you won."

She smiled. "In that, we are in complete agreement."

Epilogue

Two Years Later

"We're going to be late," Kate called.

"I'm ready," Reed said.

Kate looked up to find Reed standing by the hotel bed in his dark suit. Although it had been two years since the end of the dating challenge, her stomach fluttered like the first time they'd met. She finished latching her shoes and stood.

"You look great in a tux," she said.

"You look better in that dress," he replied.

She smiled and picked up her purse. Reed grabbed the keys to the car and collected the wedding present before opening the door. The sight of him standing on the threshold of the hotel room brought her to a halt.

He stood with his hand in his pocket, standing against the doorframe as he waited for her. His stance accentuated his torso and hips, reminded her of what lay beneath the suit. She looked him up and down and shivered.

"What?" he asked.

"Just thinking about what I get to do with you."

171

He laughed. "It's been a year since our wedding. You still feel that way?"

"Yes," she said emphatically.

She closed the gap and leaned up for a kiss—which quickly grew passionate. He dropped the present and held her against him, her hands searching inside his jacket. Breathing hard, she pulled away and glanced to the bed.

"You *sure* we don't have time?"

He grimaced. "We're already late," he said.

Logic warred with desire but this time logic won. She sighed and picked up the present. "After?" she asked.

"I promise," he said.

A slow fire burned in his eyes. She smiled and consoled herself with the fact that they would be returning to the hotel after the wedding. They left the room behind and made their way to the parking lot. Reed opened the door of the car that had once been hers, and was now theirs. He smiled as he helped her inside, keeping her dress from brushing the ground. Then he circled the car and claimed the driver's seat.

It was their first time back in Boulder in a while, and things looked different. Spring was in full swing, sunlight dancing across lilies and tulips rising from flower beds next to houses. Several buildings were new, and she marveled that it no longer felt like home.

"It feels different," he said.

"I was thinking the same thing," she said. "It's been what? A year and a half?"

He nodded. "We came back halfway through my internship," he said.

They passed the stadium and she reached out for his hand, touching the wedding band on his finger. It seemed like a lifetime ago when he'd proposed, but the memory had yet to dim. She could never have imagined what would follow.

172

Just a day after the proposal they'd flown to New York together. She'd dropped out of her classes in Boulder and, with Dr. Dickson's help, been accepted into NYU for the summer semester. She'd moved into Elaina's apartment to be her roommate, and quickly became friends.

Reed's internship had gone smoothly after Kate's arrival, and when it came time to move on, he'd gone to NYU. The two were now approaching graduation, with Reed hoping to return to the institute as a doctor.

The biggest surprise had been Hannah. The first few months after Kate's arrival, the girl had kept her distance. Despite Kate's lingering hostility towards her, the two gradually became friends, a friendship made easier when Hannah found a boyfriend.

Returning to Boulder, the birthplace of the dating challenge, brought back a wealth of memories. Reed glanced her way and turned down their old streets, passing the houses they'd once called home.

"Any regrets?" he asked.

"One," she said.

"Really?" he asked. "What's that?"

"I still think I won the challenge."

He burst into a laugh and shook his head. "The people made their choice."

"I still say you stacked the crowd in your favor," she said with a smile.

"Maybe," he said, his blue eyes twinkling.

They turned the next corner and headed east, to the city gardens, a place known for spring weddings. The parking lot was nearly full. Reed claimed one of the last spots and turned off the car, just as the final spot was filled.

"Good thing we didn't stay in the room," he said with a wink.

"I still say we had time."

He grinned and they got out. Walking hand in hand, they made their way to the front gates and into the gardens. Towering trees provided shade from the late morning sun. A slight breeze pulled at the branches, rustling the leaves. Thousands of flowers blanketed the slopes and beds, the colors diverse and bright. It was Friday and the gardens were full, so they worked their way to the wedding pavilion on the north end.

When they reached it they spotted Marta, and Kate stepped into a hug. "Where's Bake?" she asked.

"Getting me a drink," Marta said, craning her neck and then pointing. "There he is."

Baker appeared as if from nowhere and handed Marta a glass. Then he hugged Kate and nodded to Reed, who shook his hand. Kate hadn't seen him since her own wedding, when he'd been the one to give her away.

"This doesn't mean that I like you," Baker said, but his smile would not be constrained.

"Yes it does," Reed replied.

"Where are the bride and groom?" Kate asked.

Marta motioned through the crowd, where the happy couple were standing at the end of the greeting line. The wedding would be later in the evening, and this was just a reception for close family and friends.

"I'm just glad we finally got here," Marta said. "It took forever for them to pick a date."

The bride spotted them and rushed over, engulfing Kate in a hug. "I'm so happy you made it!" she cried.

"Brittney," Reed said, stepping into his own hug. "You look gorgeous."

Caleb joined them, his smile wide through his beard. "That's what I told her."

Jackson and Shelby appeared with Ember and Wilson, her current boyfriend, the longest relationship she'd ever had, and one Kate hoped would endure. Tanner had been good, but his quiet nature had eventually been too much for Ember. Wilson, on the other hand, had a sense of humor that somehow managed to defuse Ember's anger with a sly smile and a few words.

Kate and Reed greeted them all, the round of hugs and congratulations excited and happy. The five couples stood together for the first time in a year and a half, not since Kate and Reed's wedding, and Kate savored the moment.

"We *have* to get a picture together," Brittney said.

Caleb ushered them into a line, with Brittney and Caleb in the center. Kate smiled for the picture, struck by the profound sense of gratitude. The scene was a reminder of her own wedding with Reed.

"Should we tell them?" Reed whispered into her ear.

"Later," she murmured. "This is Brittney's day."

Reed's hand snaked over her belly, a reminder of the secret they had yet to share. They exchanged a look, his expression tender. She sighed and placed her hand on his, her smile spreading across her face.

"Are you ready to tell them?" he asked.

"They're family." She smiled softly. "I can't wait."

She noticed Reed's eyes on Jackson, who kept disrupting the photographer by making faces. "Do you think he'll be like his namesake?"

"If we're lucky," she said with a laugh.

Kate's gaze swept the group, of family and friends together, of the reminder of the past and a hope for a bright future. Four years ago she never would have imagined such joy lay around the corner.

"Do you think he'll mind us using his name?" Reed asked.

"I think he'll be honored," she said, her hand on her belly.

175

Brittney noticed the position of her hand and her eyes widened. She all but slapped Caleb, who turned. Brittney leveled an accusing finger at Kate. Others quickly noticed and Kate dropped her hand, but it was too late. Then Ember raised an eyebrow.

"Anything you want to tell us?"

"It's Brittney's day," Kate hedged.

"Not if you're going to say what I think," Brittney scoffed. "Now dish."

The forceful command brought a grin to everyone, and Kate glanced to Reed. He merely shrugged and pointed to her. "It's your news to share."

Kate, her stomach fluttering, smiled. "Let's just say that a new challenge is about to begin . . ."

27 Dates: The Series

The Dating Challenge

The Dating Secret

The Dating Game

The Christmas Date

The Valentine's Date

Author Bio

Originally from Utah, Ben has grown up with a passion for learning. While still young, he practiced various sports, became an Eagle Scout, and taught himself to play the piano. As a teenager he began creative dating and continued the practice into college, where he took a break to do volunteer work in Brazil. After school, he launched his first series, The Chronicles of Lumineia, and has since published over 20 titles across multiple genres. He loves to snowboard, build treehouses, and play board games, especially with his family. His greatest support and inspiration comes from his wonderful wife and six beautiful children. Currently he resides in Missouri while working on his Masters in Professional Writing.

To contact the author, discover more about 27 Dates, or find out about the upcoming sequels, check out his website at 27Dates.com. You can also follow the author on twitter @27Dates or Facebook.

www.ingramcontent.com/pod-product-compliance
Lightning Source LLC
Chambersburg PA
CBHW022120170626
46808CB00002B/782